Peril Among the Pansies

A Clover Haven Mystery

Kristy T Dixon

Copyright © 2025 by Kristy T Dixon

All rights reserved.

No part of this publication may be reproduced, distributed, or transmitted in any form or by any means, including photocopying, recording, or other electronic or mechanical methods, without the prior written permission of the publisher, except as permitted by U.S. copyright law. For permission requests, contact kristydixon35@gmail.com.

The story, all names, characters, and incidents portrayed in this production are fictitious. No identification with actual persons (living or deceased), places, buildings, and products is intended or should be inferred.

Book Cover by Mariah Sinclair

Edited by E-race Editing

For Faunice, Erin, and Jessica

Chapter 1

I tried to keep my face pleasant as the teen boy in front of the counter squirmed. No matter how many times this happened, it never ceased to amaze me.

I glanced at the wilted corsage he'd placed on the counter and then back at him. "You bought a corsage a week ago, and the dance is tonight?" I finally asked.

He shifted from one foot to the other. "Yeah. I kept it in the fridge, but it still got all brown and ugly."

"You can only keep flowers for twenty-four hours. They'll never last a week, even in the fridge."

He raked his hand through his curly brown hair and frowned. "You should probably have a sign that says that or something."

I pointed at a framed sign that said exactly that.

He sighed. "Well, you should probably tell people in case they don't see the sign."

"Most people know that once you cut flowers, they start to die."

"So, there's nothing you can do...?"

I sighed and looked at the ceiling. In reality, I always kept extra flowers around on weekends with school dances, because, without fail, there was a handful of kids who didn't know they had to order in advance. I always gave them a bit of a hard time so they'd plan better next time, but I didn't want anyone to have to go to a dance without a corsage.

I ran the only flower shop in the county, and that made me popular during certain times of the year. The county's population wasn't big, but there were still plenty of people to keep me in business.

"I might have something in the back."

He beamed. "Thank you!"

I slipped into the cooler and grabbed a corsage—white instead of red, but better than nothing. I didn't want to punish kids, just give them a little life lesson about being prepared.

I came back out and showed it to him. "I have this. Will it work?"

He nodded. "Anything is better than a dead one. Thanks. What do I owe you?"

"Hmm," I said, tapping my lip. "I'll give you a two-dollar discount, but don't expect me to help you like this again."

"Thanks!" His eyes lit up. "I'm going to tell all my friends to get their flowers here!" He grabbed the corsage, slammed some money on the counter, and hurried away.

"You do that," I muttered, throwing the dead corsage in the trash under the counter.

I didn't need word of mouth. With no other options, everyone came to me. I'd started *Neeley's Flower Patch* because my grandpa owned the only mortuary in the county. People always complained about the stress of getting flowers, so I'd built my business on the same property as the mortuary.

The mortuary wasn't too close to my shop, but a short drive down the road and up a hill. You would never think the properties were owned by the same person. My shop was bright and cute, and the mortuary looked like a small version of Dracula's Castle. Most mortuaries are modern-looking, but my grandpa didn't feel like doing a remodel.

The front door burst open, and one of my two employees rushed in.

"I'm late!" Roberta said, pulling her brown hair back into a ponytail. It appeared she'd forgotten to brush it. "Sorry."

"Only five minutes. It's not a problem."

"Tonight is prom. I'm guessing we're going to be busy."

"We're well stocked if we are."

I hired Roberta and Jessa five years ago when I opened, and they were the best employees a person could have.

It was only 9:05, and my long, dark brown hair was already beginning to fall out of the messy bun I'd thrown together this morning. I tried pushing some of it back into place, but it was a wreck.

"It's supposed to rain tonight," Roberta informed me. "You should have gotten the roof fixed."

"I'll fix it today."

"You should call a professional."

"I Googled it. I've been watching videos on how to fix it all week."

Roberta put her hands on her ample waist and frowned. "We don't need you falling and breaking something."

Sometimes I wondered if she had appointed herself my honorary mother. Of course, Jessa was the same. They both tried to look out for me, and they liked to remind me they had a lot more life experience than I did.

"The roof isn't high. It'll be fine."

"I'll put the sheriff on speed dial while you're up there."

I cringed. "Do not call the sheriff, even if I fall on my head."

"Why not? Sheriff McGregor is the best sheriff this county has ever seen. And man, is that boy funny."

I smiled. "Boy? He's thirty-five."

"When you're fifty-five, thirty-five is a boy."

"Who are we talking about?" Jessa asked, coming in from the back.

I jumped slightly.

Roberta smiled at her. "Sheriff McGregor."

Jessa's face lit up. "Honey, if I were twenty years younger, I would be dating that man." She grabbed some ribbon and began measuring it. "Why are we talking about the sheriff?"

"I told Neeley I was going to call him if she fell off the roof," Roberta repeated.

Jessa fixed me with a stare. "And why are you going on the roof?"

"It has a leak… and it's going to rain." I felt like a kid caught sneaking cookies, fumbling to explain myself.

Jessa put down her scissors and rubbed one of her small black braids between her fingers. "Ask the sheriff to fix it. That man's handy. Handy and handsome." She laughed, and Roberta joined in.

I rolled my eyes and grabbed a ribbon to tie around a boutonniere. "If I waited around for someone else to fix things, I'd be waiting forever. Besides, I'm not helpless."

It was true. I wasn't. My grandpa had raised me, and he was a very busy man. That meant any problem that came up over the years, I figured out myself. I had more skills than I knew what to do with sometimes. I'd had my share of bruises and bad calls, but that was how you learn. Trial by leaking faucet.

"Uh oh," Roberta teased. "Neeley's going to go off on her man rant."

I smiled. "I'm not against men. I just know what I can do." I could admit it might be nice to have someone who could help me with things like fixing the roof, but since I didn't, there wasn't a reason to wish for it.

"Sheriff McGregor helped me fix my front step once," Jessa said. "Helped is the wrong word. He did it while I sat on my porch admiring his arms as he hammered." She laughed again, and so did Roberta.

Why did we have to talk about the sheriff? I could think of millions of better topics.

"Ask him," Roberta said, straightening the decorations on the counter. "Just bat your pretty blue eyes at him, and he'll do whatever you say."

I shook my head and tried to look passive. "I have other things to think about. Like what the book is going to be for book club this week? We had a vote, and it was a tie."

Jessa cut some more ribbon. "I haven't finished the last book. Every time I start on it, I get tired and fall asleep." She perked up. "Oh! Who's bringing the dessert?"

I tilted my head. "I thought it was you?"

"Right. It is my turn. I better figure it out. It's going to be hard to beat Lydia's tarts from last week."

We held our book club twice a week. It might seem obsessive, but in a town this size, people needed things to do. We read cozy murder mysteries, and we talked about them in one of the rooms in the mortuary. Some people might think that was a little morbid, but it made things a little more interesting.

The door opened, and two teenage girls entered. Roberta greeted them as I went into the back to get the boutonnieres they had ordered. I knew both girls, so I didn't need to ask why they were there.

I grabbed two plastic clamshell containers and brought them out.

Handing them to Roberta, I turned to Jessa. "I'm going to drive over to Crystal Rock and see if they have anything I can use to patch the roof. Call me if you need anything."

"Sure thing," Jessa said. "Make sure you take your jacket. It might rain."

I nodded and grabbed it off the hook by the door. I'd learned that arguing with Jessa and Roberta about some things was pointless. One of those things was wearing a jacket. The weather was usually around seventy degrees, but they were always fussing about jackets. I didn't remember my mom very well, but I doubted she would have been as bossy as these two.

I climbed into my red Mazda and tossed the jacket on the passenger's seat. Crystal Rock was overpriced, overhyped, and thirty minutes too far—but it had the nearest hardware store. Clover Haven also had a small convenience store, but unless you wanted an overpriced single serving of chips, it was best to avoid it. Once a month, I drove even farther to stock up in the city. But today wasn't a big trip. Just roof stuff. Annoying roof stuff.

There was only one way from Clover Haven to Crystal Rock, but once I got to town, I took a strange roundabout way to the store. I told myself it was for the view, but really, I just didn't want to pass Troy's place. Fifteen years should've been long enough to stop caring where he lived, but apparently, I was still working on that. He probably didn't live there anymore, anyway.

The rain had started as a mist but turned into a steady drizzle, the kind that made the world look like it had been painted in watercolors. The pavement shone dark and slick, and magnolia petals clung to branches like silk scarves that didn't want to let go.

I didn't turn on the radio. Too many of those songs knew exactly where to aim. One wrong lyric, and I'd be thinking about the first time I saw him in his stupid green hoodie. And that was not a road I had time to go down.

I shook my head and turned onto the main road. Think about the roof. Or Grandpa. Anything but Troy.

Grandpa had always been gruff in a sweet, grizzly-bear way, but lately... I was starting to worry. His mind remained sharp... mostly... but he'd been imagining things. At least, I thought he was imagining them.

He kept calling the police, saying someone was breaking into the mortuary, sneaking around, and stealing things. It happened almost weekly now. I'd checked every time—no forced entry, nothing missing—but he swore someone had been there. Said he heard them.

I wanted to believe it was nothing, but the police were getting fed up. They had to drive all the way out from Crystal Rock and waste an hour round-trip to tell him everything was fine. I'd tried explaining that no one had been inside, but it always ended in an argument. And I hated fighting with him.

I managed to get in and out of the hardware store without seeing anyone from my past. I did spot a truck marked 'Sheriff' in the parking lot but avoided it like the plague. If Troy was in town, odds were good he was behind the wheel. No, thank you.

Another thirty minutes later, I pulled back into the lot behind my flower shop. Mission accomplished. Supplies purchased, feelings mostly stuffed. All in all, not a bad trip.

I got out of the car and admired my shop. Even after all this time, I still stopped to take in the little place I'd built. The one-story building had a gleaming front window that flooded the space with sunshine. A fancy glass door sat just off-center, framed by perfectly neat white trim. Above the door was a wooden sign that said *Neeley's Flower Patch*, with a picture of a bouquet. Flowers bloomed all around the outside of the shop. It only seemed fitting.

If you were close enough, you could see a bright bouquet in the window that changed every few days.

I opened the door and gazed around. There was a small reception area, and then a few feet into the small rectangular room, there was a long counter that we could stand behind. Shelves and stands ran around the walls, and all were covered in flowers, both real and fake.

Jessa was at the front counter arguing with a woman about something. It wasn't a shock. Billie Patterson argued about everything and was probably the reason book club always went over.

I slipped into the back and put my bags in the corner. I'd get to the roof after lunch.

Roberta was sitting at a long table that we used to put together bouquets. That was what we used the back room for. The floral coolers were in here—and all the supplies we needed to put things together. We'd decorated it with wreaths that weren't exactly worthy of being sold. It made the room cheerier.

"I lucked out and was in the back when Billie came in," Roberta said. "Jessa deals with her better than I can."

"I wonder if she buys so many flowers just so she can come in and argue."

"I wouldn't doubt it. She seems to thrive on it. Did you get what you need?"

"Yeah. I don't think it should be a hard fix. I only had this place built five years ago. The roof shouldn't be having major problems already."

"Your grandpa called while you were gone. He said you weren't answering your cell."

I sighed. "I was driving. Did he tell you what he wanted?"

"He said there's someone hiding in the morgue. He said not to worry, he called the police."

"I don't understand what's happening," I said, sitting down to help with the bouquet. "He doesn't act senile except with this one thing. I don't understand what he thinks he's hearing. And he keeps telling me someone is stealing things. When I ask what things, he just mumbles something and leaves the room." I rubbed my forehead and considered my options.

"And you haven't seen anything missing?"

"No." I worked at the mortuary as well as at my shop. I dealt with all the paperwork, so I got it done whenever I had time. I also lived in a room there, so I was around enough that I thought I would notice if things went missing.

"He works hard. Maybe the stress is getting to him."

"It could be. He still remembers all his appointments, and he does good work. That's why I think it's odd he's so fixated on this."

"I want to see the owner!" Billie yelled from the other room.

I rolled my eyes and stood. "I guess I'll go help Jessa out. I'll be right back."

"Hey, Billie," I said when I walked out. "What's up?"

"You raised the price of your orchids by an entire dollar." She straightened her pink blouse and glared.

"Prices go up, unfortunately," I said.

"But by a dollar? All at once?"

"Sometimes."

"You sound like my hairdresser. I've been going to that woman weekly for the last ten years, and suddenly a perm costs five dollars more."

"You go to the hairdresser every week?" Jessa asked, her eyes wide.

"Yes. I get a perm once a week, then I don't ever have to do my hair," she said, touching her short, gray curls. "You shouldn't look surprised. You told me it takes eight hours to get your braids in."

Jessa shrugged. "True, but I don't have to do it that often."

"So, what about the price?" She crossed her arms and glared expectantly.

I shrugged. "What about it?"

"Are you going to fix it?"

"Sorry. I have to make a profit or I'll go out of business. When I get charged more for supplies, I have to raise prices."

"Fine, I'll pay the extra dollar," she muttered and tossed some cash on the counter.

Jessa took it and smiled, handing her a blue orchid.

"I guess you can charge anything you want since you have no competition."

I gave her a tight smile. "If you check online, you'll see that my prices are competitive for similar places in Southern California."

Billie grabbed the flower. "Where's my change?"

"You were actually a few cents short," Jessa said.

Her eyes narrowed. "I wasn't short."

"You didn't account for sales tax."

"Wow, you people nickel and dime a woman." She turned and stomped from the room, the flower clutched in her hand. The door slammed behind her.

I looked at Jessa, and we burst out laughing. That was pretty much the way dealing with Billie went. I might've felt bad, but Billie's family had money, and paying an extra dollar wasn't going to hurt her bank account.

Chapter 2

I didn't know what had caused the hole in the flower shop roof, but something had punched straight through a shingle. Having a flat roof made it easy to work on. I'd removed the broken shingle, patched the hole underneath, and just nailed down a new one. It wasn't the prettiest job, but it would hold—and no one could see it from the ground, anyway.

I stood and nodded. It was fine.

"What are you doing up there?"

My heart jumped to my throat, and my back stiffened. I might not have heard that voice in fifteen years, but I still knew it. Running and diving off the back wasn't an option. Not unless I wanted to break an ankle.

I turned and glared down at the man staring up at me. "What do you want, Sheriff?" I asked.

His frown deepened. "You shouldn't be up there. You might fall."

"I won't fall."

He tilted his head and put his hands on his hips. "Can you come down here and talk for a minute?"

I sighed. There were no good excuses. The roof was finished, but I was not in the mood to talk to him. I tossed all my garbage down—and my hammer. I threw it as close to him as I could without actually hitting him. I might have been trying to make him nervous, but he didn't so much as flinch.

I climbed onto the ladder and frowned when he held it steady. I'd gotten up here without trouble. I didn't need help to get down, especially not from him. When I got to the bottom, I brushed off my pants and avoided looking into his perfect green eyes.

"Are you going to talk?" I asked, looking slightly over his shoulder.

"Your grandpa keeps calling the police. I'm having trouble getting any officers to come here because they all know it's a waste of time."

"And what do you want me to do, Sheriff?"

I finally looked at him and immediately regretted it. I should have known the best-looking guy in high school would grow up to be the best-looking guy ever. He'd always been in shape, but time had only sharpened the lines of his jaw and shoulders. Thirty-five suited him in an in-furiating way.

His eyes narrowed. "You don't have to call me—listen, you need to talk to your grandpa. Maybe get him some medical help."

I tried to ignore the way his sandy blond hair fell over his forehead like he'd just come out of a windstorm. He needed a haircut. Troy McGregor had always had looks that seemed unfair for everyone else, and he hadn't lost that in the years since I'd seen him.

His tan button-up shirt looked like it was tailored for his broad shoulders and the knees in his jeans were worn enough that one more kneel might finish them off.

It wasn't a bad look on him. It was odd seeing the shiny badge attached to his shirt.

"I know," I said, realizing I hadn't answered. "He won't go. He seems fine except for thinking someone is in the mortuary."

"I can't waste resources and officers on coming out here every week."

"So don't send anyone."

"We can't ignore calls. Then if something actually happened and we didn't respond, we would be in trouble."

"I can't help you."

He sighed. "Will you go up with me to talk to him?"

I raised my eyebrow. "You really want to talk to him? He hates you."

"He always has."

"Yeah, but the years have made him hate you more."

He took a deep breath and nodded. "I still need to talk to him."

"Fine. Let's go." I turned and walked around the flower shop and figured he was following. There was a trail in the weeds that went from the shop to the mortuary, because I went up so often and I rarely took the time to get my car.

I felt funny knowing he was behind me. I should have told him to take his truck and meet me there. It was only a five-minute walk, but knowing he was back there made me self-conscious.

I regretted not taking more time to style my hair this morning. My green shirt and jeans were cute, so I at least had that going for me. I resisted the urge to pull out my bun. My hair was one of my favorite things about myself, but if I did, it meant I was trying to get him to notice, and why would I want that?

"How's Chase?" I finally asked to break the awkward silence.

"He's good. He got married recently."

My stomach fell a little. "Good for him. Anyone I know?" I might have some old grudges from the past, but they weren't against Chase.

"No. She recently moved here."

I nodded and kept walking. Chase had been one of my best friends for a long time, and I wished him the best. As for Troy... I wasn't sure what I wished for him. Maybe to slip and fall on his face.

I knew I wasn't being fair. Troy hadn't really done anything to me. I'd come to realize over the years that I'd probably overreacted and ruined the only two friendships I'd ever cared about, but it had been so long now, I felt like I had to stay bitter.

"Don't you want to know what I've been up to?" Troy asked.

I shrugged. "Being sheriff, I assume."

He didn't say anything. I was glad I couldn't see his face.

I sighed. "So, what have you been up to, Sheriff McGregor?"

"You can call me Troy."

"Hmm. I think I need to keep saying 'sheriff.' You have to realize it was a bit of a shock when you, of all people, became sheriff. I need to say it to remind myself you aren't just the town riffraff anymore."

He caught my arm and gently pulled me to a stop.

I turned and glared at him.

"The town riffraff? Really, Neeley? Any trouble I caused was with you and Chase, and we never did anything that bad. Besides, we all grew up. At least I figured we did."

His green eyes pierced mine, and I swallowed. I couldn't figure out why I was going out of my way to be a jerk. In reality, I knew he was a great sheriff. Everyone loved him.

It was hard to live here and not overhear people sing his praise.

I pulled my arm away and continued walking. Troy broke my heart fifteen years ago, but it wasn't fair of me to treat him this way. He hadn't known I'd fallen in love with him. He still didn't know. I wasn't in love with him anymore, of course. Fifteen years was a long time.

"I wish we could have a talk about what happened," he said. "I'm still not sure why you were so mad."

My mouth turned down. I didn't want to be nice, so I needed to stop talking. "I don't want to talk about it."

"Fine, but I think it's sad you ruined two long friendships because you listened to a liar over your best friends."

Troy, Chase, and I had been inseparable since kindergarten. We were the kind of trio that pulled harmless pranks, laughed at everything, and thought the world revolved around our friendship. Chase and Troy were good-looking, athletic, and charming, and they knew it.

By the time we hit sixteen, something shifted. My harmless friend-crush on Troy had turned into something more, and every time I watched girls try to flirt with him, it grated on my nerves. He and Chase didn't date anyone seriously, but they never lacked attention. Eventually, something happened. I got angry, I overreacted, and I let everything fall apart.

"Sorry, Neeley. I shouldn't have said that."

I kept walking.

"It's nice you made your dream of owning a flower shop come true," he said.

I swallowed. I didn't want to talk to Troy. I didn't need old regret and stupid feelings keeping me up at night. I might be over him, but he was the reason I barely dated. I compared everyone to him, and it wasn't fair. Not everyone can be Troy McGregor.

"It sounds like your shop does well," he said.

I rolled my eyes. "You don't need to talk to fill the air. We don't know each other."

"I talk to most people I'm with."

We went up to the tall door of the mortuary, and I pulled it open.

"Wow, I have some good memories about this place," he said. "Remember when we used to play ghost in the graveyard here?"

I ignored him as we entered. The receptionist's desk was empty, which wasn't odd. My uncle Jerry usually answered the phones, but we had a cell number, so he didn't have to sit at the desk. There really wasn't a lot to do here. Jerry also did all the make-up on the corpses who came through. This was a family business. That was how my grandpa liked it. He would have everyone who worked here be family, but he couldn't get enough relatives to come, so he'd had to hire others.

"Grandpa?" I called, my voice echoing around the dreary lobby.

"It all looks exactly like it did the last time I was here," Troy said.

"Grandpa isn't into spending money on making things look nice. I wish he would tear the place down and build a nice modern building, but he's against that. This one is too big and gloomy. He said it's not a big deal because he doesn't have any competition."

"That sounds like Walt. I always loved this place, though."

"Grandpa!" I yelled. Looking for someone in this place was ridiculous. It could take forever, and my grandpa refused to keep his phone with him so I could ask where he was.

"What's wrong, Neeley?" my grandpa asked, coming through a side door. "I'm getting ready to embalm someone."

Troy chuckled.

My grandpa's eyes fell on him. "What are you doing here?" he growled.

Troy shrugged. "You called."

"Yeah, and every time I call, I deliberately tell them to send anyone but Troy McGregor. But here you are anyway."

"Sorry. You've worn out all my officers, so you're stuck with me."

He blew out a breath. "Fine. Someone's been snooping around, I can't catch them. I want them out. I'm a busy man, and I can't be chasing after crooks. If you find them, you can let me know." He turned to leave.

"Wait, Mr. Kelter?" Troy said. "Can you give me more to go on?"

"Have to have everything fed to you, eh?"

Troy ignored him. "I need to know where you're hearing things and what makes you think someone is here."

"I hear things fall, and things disappear. Just look around and figure it out."

Troy nodded, and I ignored the gleam in his eyes. My grandpa was never nice to Troy or Chase. He thought they were a bad influence on me, and they had always found him amusing.

"Come with me, Neeley," Grandpa said. "I don't want you alone with this man."

"I need to go back to the shop," I protested. "I just fixed the roof and need to get some things together for tomorrow."

"I'll walk you out," he said, taking my arm. He looked at Troy. "As for you, get to work."

Troy saluted and left the room. He could navigate this place with his eyes shut. We'd spend a lot of time playing games here.

We walked out, and Grandpa turned to me. "I hope he didn't upset you."

"No. Why would he?"

"You never told me what happened that ruined your friendship, but I know he's rotten."

"He's not rotten. We just drifted apart."

He scratched his gray hair and frowned. "Drifting apart means a gradual process. You dropped him and Chase overnight. It took you weeks before you weren't upset, so I'm sure there was something to it."

"It doesn't matter. It's all fine." I kissed his cheek. "Go do your embalming. I have some stuff to get finished."

"Alright, but if that man upsets you again, he better be ready to fight."

I laughed. "Good to know."

My grandpa was about five foot eight and two hundred and fifty pounds. None of that was muscle. He was also close to eighty and didn't move as fast as he once did. He wouldn't get anywhere fighting Troy, but it was nice to know he thought he had my back. I smiled to myself, even if it didn't reach my lips.

Chapter 3

I pulled some petals from a few roses and glared at them. They were too far gone to sell. That was the second time this month I'd had shipments with unusable flowers. It irritated me, but what could I do? I tossed them in the trash and looked at what else I had to work with.

Someone had come into the shop and was talking to Roberta and Jessa. I couldn't hear what they were saying, but they kept laughing.

I smiled. Having Jessa and Roberta around was good for me. They found things funny that weren't—and sometimes that was a good thing. I was prone to focusing on the serious side of things these days.

I grabbed some daisies and stuffed them into the bouquet I was making. It wouldn't be as good without the roses, but I could make something decent. I added some baby's breath to the sides and nodded. It would be decorating someone's table soon.

The vase was heavy, so I picked it up and carefully walked it out to the display room in the store. I forced myself not to scowl when the person who had come in turned out to be Troy McGregor. He was telling a story with exaggerated motions, and Jessa and Roberta were hanging on to his every word. His eyes shone as he talked, and I looked away.

I placed the bouquet on the counter and grabbed a card to stick inside.

"Good morning, Neeley," Troy said, the humor gone from his eyes.

I nodded. "Sheriff." I tried to keep my expression neutral, but my insides were in peril. Troy almost looked the same as he had at twenty, but something heavier lingered in his expression.

I was glad I'd worn my hair down today. And I hated that I cared.

"Sheriff Troy was telling us the funniest story," Roberta said. She turned to him. "You should tell it again so Neeley can hear it."

"I need to get things ready for the funeral tomorrow," I said. "Maybe another time." I turned and went to the back room.

I heard the front door close, and I sighed with relief.

Jessa walked in and put her hands on her hips. "What was that?"

"Excuse me?"

"Why are you so cold to the sheriff?"

"I wasn't cold. I just didn't want to hear his dumb story."

"It wasn't dumb. It was funny."

I grabbed a flower and wound it into a wreath. "If you want to listen to him, that's fine. He puts me in a bad mood."

"Why is that?"

I shrugged and kept filling the wreath with flowers.

Roberta came in next and grabbed some red ribbon. "I'm surprised the sheriff isn't married. He's funny, handsome, and so nice. All the young women in town talk about him. We should try to set him up with someone."

"That's a good idea," Jessa said. "Do you have someone in mind?"

"Hmm. What about Abigail Perkins?"

"No way. She bites her nails." Jessa snorted.

"That's not a big deal."

Jessa raised her brow. "Sure, but she spits them out all over the place, and that's just gross. How about Millie? She's around his age."

Roberta wrinkled her nose. "I don't see the two of them together."

I rolled my eyes and kept working.

Jessa gave a small laugh. "I would say Neeley, but I don't think she's interested."

Roberta giggled. "They would look great together, wouldn't they?"

I sighed and didn't look up. "Never in a hundred years," I grumbled.

"What do you have against the sheriff?" Roberta asked. "I'm sure he has flaws, but I'm not seeing any of them."

I kept working and didn't answer. I'd wanted to spill my frustrations about Troy to someone for years, but I didn't feel comfortable doing it, especially not to two members of his fan club. Troy and Chase had always been the people I confided in, and that had left me with fifteen years of only taking my own advice.

"Do you ever date?" Jessa asked. "If you have, I've never heard of it."

"Nope."

"Any reason?"

I shrugged. "Not one I want to talk about. And why are you two bugging me about it? Do the two of you date?"

Roberta laughed. "Every chance I get. Of course, there aren't a lot of men around here who interest me. I've gone into the city a few times to meet guys I met online."

Jessa shook her head, her black braids swaying. "When my husband died, I didn't feel like remarrying. This isn't about us. It's about you. Tell us why you don't date."

I threaded a flower through some leaves and swallowed. I didn't want to admit to being bitter and stuck in the past. "You know there are some crazy people who only fall in love once?"

"That's me," Jessa said.

I nodded. "Me too. I fell in love. It was a one-way thing. He disappointed me, but I can't stop comparing every guy I meet to him. I stopped trying. I'm better off on my own."

"That's depressing," Roberta said.

I gave her a small, forced smile. "I'm happy with my life. I don't need anyone feeling bad for me."

"Do we need any more wreaths to sell online?" Jessa asked.

We'd started selling wreaths and other decorations with fake flowers because it gave us something to do when things were slow.

"We could use one or two more."

"I'll start on that."

"Great." I wondered why just talking about Troy was making my heart pound. Memo to me: Troy was last decade's news.

⚘

Someone was in the attic. I stared at the ceiling and listened to the soft footsteps. My heart stopped, and I stayed glued to my bed. My room was on the top floor of the three-story mortuary, and I'd never heard anyone up there. The only people who lived in the building were my grandpa and uncle.

There was no way one of them was in the attic. Neither one of them would be able to get up there without a lot of effort. There was only one way in, and it involved having a ladder or being really good at jumping and pulling your weight up through the small hole in the ceiling.

When I was a teenager, I used to go up there with Troy and Chase, but it had been years since I'd stepped foot up there.

Sitting up, I tried not to let the shadows in my room scare me. Calling the police was the smart option, but it would take them thirty minutes to get here. Anything could happen in that much time.

I climbed out of bed, stepped into my fuzzy blue slippers, and grabbed my robe. Maybe Grandpa hadn't been imagining things.

I grabbed the baseball bat near my door and tiptoed out of my room. The top floor was where we lived. This floor's layout included bedrooms, bathrooms, a kitchen, living room, and laundry, all accessible via one long, dark hallway. I didn't want to turn on the light and risk warning whoever was up there, or worse, waking Grandpa. There was no need for him to be searching. What could he do anyway?

At the end of the hallway, I stopped and looked up. It was hard to see with only my phone light, but the attic access appeared to be tightly shut. Of course, as someone who used to go up there when I wasn't supposed to, I knew it was easier to make it look untouched from inside the attic than from down here.

The attic was the perfect place for kids, and I always thought it was a pity Grandpa didn't want us up there. To get up, one of my friends would have to boost me. Then I would push it open and they would toss me straight up, or I'd step in their hand and they would push up. We'd hidden a ladder inside, so I would lower it for them, then we would pull it up, so no one knew. Now that I thought about it, we were probably lucky no one ever got hurt.

Inside the attic was a large room, and then the best thing—the turrets. There were two of them. One on each side. That was what made the mortuary look like a castle. The two towers protruding from the building were the best clubhouses a kid could have. Grandpa forbade me from playing in them, but we'd still done it.

They were purely for decoration, but they both had small spiral staircases that went up to a small, round room. Chase, Troy, and I had spent hours in them, playing board games or doing homework. I hadn't been up in over fifteen years, because it was too hard to access. If someone were in the attic now, I couldn't see how they'd managed to get up.

No light shined through the cracks of the trapdoor, so I decided to go outside to see if I could see anything in the towers or the small, round attic windows. No one would be up there with no light. There would be no point.

The floor creaked as I walked, and I did my best to ignore the chill running down my spine. I turned to the big staircase and began my slow descent. Taking even breaths, I kept my grip on my phone and the baseball bat.

When I got to the bottom, I rushed through the hall and across the lobby. I was more scared than I wanted to admit.

I left the safety of the building, and the cool air slapped me in the face. I hurried down the stairs and far enough from the structure to look at it critically.

The towers and the attic windows were dark...

I must have been imagining things. All Grandpa's talk about noises was getting to me. It was also possible we had an animal up there. It had happened before. Still, I felt like I'd heard footsteps... which could have been part of a half-asleep dream.

I couldn't think of any reason or way a person had gotten up there, so I went back in. I jumped when I walked into the lobby and saw something behind the desk.

"Who's there?" I demanded, holding up the bat.

The desk light flipped on, and my Uncle Jerry stood at the desk in his pajamas.

I put a hand to my heart. "Dang it! You scared me to death."

Jerry chuckled. "What are you doing with a bat? And outside at this time?"

"I thought I heard something in the attic."

Jerry rubbed a hand over his gray hair. "And you thought going outside with a bat would help? That's far from the attic."

"I was checking to see if there were any lights on."

"Were there?"

"No."

"I bet it's another raccoon. We should cut down all the big trees that grow near the roof."

"It sounded like footsteps." I shook my head. "I bet I was just dreaming. Grandpa's got me wound up."

Jerry sighed. "I'm not sure what to do about him. I hope he isn't losing his mind."

"He isn't having any other problems except hearing things."

"And thinking things are going missing."

I placed the top of the bat against the floor and turned it around absentmindedly. "Have you noticed anything missing?"

"No. I hate to say it, but I think it might be time to get some medical help for Dad."

I frowned and kept spinning the bat. I'd been thinking the same thing, but it made me nervous. If a doctor said something was wrong, I was going to have to accept that, and I wasn't ready.

"He's still doing well with his job," I finally said.

"Yes, but he does lose things more than he used to. I wonder if the things he feels are missing are just misplaced. I'm sorry, Neeley, but we might have to accept that he's getting older, and his mind is going."

"What will happen to the mortuary if he can't run it?"

"You don't need to worry about that. I'm sure the two of us can handle things if it comes to that."

I nodded. "I'm going back to bed."

Jerry had worked here since he was a teenager. He had to know the way everything worked. The mortuary would go to Jerry if something happened to Grandpa. Jerry was my dad's older brother. After Jerry, it would go to me, because my aunt had moved far away and wanted nothing to do with it. I knew Grandpa wanted the mortuary to stay in the family, but I wasn't sure I could run it as well as my flower shop if it came to that.

"Goodnight," Jerry said as I scurried away.

When I got to my bed, I listened hard for more footsteps, but I didn't hear any. I wasn't sure how long I tried to sleep. My ears were ready for anything, and it was difficult to relax. With no more noise to bother me, I was letting the eerie silence unsettle me.

By morning, I was exhausted.

When I got to my shop, Roberta and Jessa were already there.

"Sorry," I said, hurrying in. I dropped my purse in a drawer under the register and inspected the shop. Everything was in order.

"You're never late," Roberta said. "Bad night? You look exhausted."

I shrugged. "I let something scare me last night, then I couldn't sleep."

Jessa shivered. "I don't know how you live in that place. It looks like a haunted house, and the inside isn't any better than the outside."

"I've always lived there, so I guess I'm used to it. I used to scare myself a lot when I was younger, but it's been a while."

"Have you ever thought of moving out?"

"No. I need to take care of my grandpa. Besides, I have a huge room, and my room has been redone, so it looks more modern. My closet is almost the size of this room."

Roberta smiled. "And we all know that's important."

Jessa tilted her head. "You care about that kind of thing?"

"You know I don't," Roberta said. "But Neeley is always stylish. Me? I've had this shirt for at least ten years, and it's been looking tattered for at least three. Shopping is not my hobby."

Jessa raised her eyebrow. "You should let me take you sometime."

They kept talking, and I grabbed a squeegee and bucket from the back so I could clean the front window. If there was one thing you could say about this shop, it was that it was spotless. With not a lot to do, some days I found myself over-cleaning so I didn't get bored.

The front window wasn't dirty, but I knew today would be slow. All the dances were over for the month, and there weren't any funerals scheduled. We would be lucky to have anyone come in for the next two or three days.

I probably should've cut the hours we were open more than they were, but I knew Jessa and Roberta needed the hours, and I had the money to keep it going even when it slowed down. My parents died in a boat crash when I was four, and all their money went to me. I didn't have to work; I did it so I wouldn't get lazy.

That wasn't the only reason. I'd always wanted a flower shop, and it was fun. Designing beautiful things felt fulfilling. Then there was my job at the morgue. It wasn't overwhelming either, and my grandpa needed me. Being busy made life keep moving.

Chapter 4

"You guys aren't eating enough," I said, looking at the book club members. "Whenever that happens, I end up with all the leftovers and have to eat them."

"You could use a few extra pounds," Jessa said, taking a bite of a gooey chocolate chip cookie.

I sat at the head of the long table and grabbed a brownie. We were up to nine members, so we could still hold three more at the table. The black table I'd purchased went with the rest of the eerie room. The walls were dusky gray, and the lights were too dim. There was a big window, but I kept the dark blinds closed. I'd even gotten an old candle holder that could hold three candles and put it in the center of the table.

We tried to pretend like we were reading things that were a little creepy, but we were all just fooling ourselves. Give us a book with a cat, a mystery, and a handsome neighbor, and we were all happy.

"Did everyone read the book?" I asked, holding my copy in the air. Everyone nodded. "What do we think?"

"I guessed the murderer as soon as he was introduced," Billie said, looking smug. That was the first thing she said at every book club.

"You did not," Jim Durbidge grumbled. Jim was our only male member so far, and he wasn't a fan of Billie.

"Sure I did. It was as obvious as anything." She straightened her blazer and patted her flower-covered hat. Some members liked to dress up for every book club. Billie called this her 'Jessica Fletcher' look.

"I don't think so," Jessa said. "I think they tried to make it look like it was the maid."

Billie rolled her eyes. "That made it too obvious that it wasn't. Besides, the maid was supposed to be five foot nothing and a thin reed of a thing. How would she hide the body of a large man? There was no way it was her."

"Was I the only one who thought the author was winging it?" Roberta asked. "I'm not sure she even knew where she was going with it until the end."

I rested my elbows on the table. "I think she planned it. If she hadn't, there wouldn't have been any clues."

"I dunno," Lydia said, tossing her dyed blond hair. "I think some authors are good at making things up as they go."

"That's how I would write," Jim said. "Who wants to follow an outline? That makes things boring."

"I thought the dog might have had something to do with it," Jessa said. "Like maybe someone was controlling him. I was sad he wasn't involved."

"We need to make sure we choose a book for next week," I said. "It's always obnoxious when we don't pick anything and I have to figure it out myself, then everyone complains."

"What if we take the top book of the day in cozy mysteries?" Jessa suggested. "Or do the first book that's recommended when you type in *cozy mystery*."

"That might be fun." I pulled out my phone to search. The problem with reading four books a month was that I liked them in paperback, so I needed to order fast so it arrived in time to read. I was a fast reader, but I needed to make sure the order didn't get delayed.

A loud pop made everyone jump.

My eyebrows came together. "What was that?"

Jim leaned forward. "Sounded like a bullet."

I stood. "I'm sure it was nothing, but will you all excuse me a minute?" I hurried from the room and into the dim gray hall. The last time I'd seen Grandpa, he'd been in his office. I hurried that way and knocked on his door.

"Grandpa?"

He didn't answer.

I pushed the door open and gasped. A man lay sprawled on the floor near the bookshelf, unmoving. Grandpa stood behind his desk, gripping a gun with both hands like he wasn't sure what to do next.

He looked at me with wide eyes. "Neeley, go call the police. Someone shot this man."

I looked from his gun to the man.

"Hurry!" he commanded.

I rushed from the room and leaned against the wall, placing a hand to my heart. Did my grandpa kill that man? That's what it looked like. I pulled out my phone and dialed Troy's number. At least the number he'd had fifteen years ago. I probably should have called 911, but I wasn't thinking clearly.

"Neeley?" Troy answered. He still had my number in his phone.

"Troy? I... I think..."

"What's wrong?"

"I think my grandpa shot someone."

There was a pause. "Are they dead?"

"I didn't check, but I think so."

"I'll send an ambulance, and I'll get there as fast as I can."

He hung up, and I stuck my phone in my pocket. I stood a few minutes, not knowing what to do, then I remembered the people here for book club.

I hurried to the room. "Hey, something has happened, and you all need to leave, and be careful."

"Was it a gun?" Jim asked.

I took a deep breath. "Can we talk about it later?"

He nodded and grabbed his cane. I led everyone to the door, trying not to think about my grandpa holding a gun.

Once everyone was gone, I went back to the office. Grandpa was still holding the gun and standing in the same place.

"Put the gun down," I told him. "The police are coming."

He looked from the gun to the man. "We have to figure out who shot him."

I stepped over the dead man and held out my hand. "Give me the gun." Dead bodies didn't bother me. I'd been around them my entire life.

He shook his head. "I need the gun in case the murderer comes back. You should get behind me."

I frowned and pointed at the desk. "If you don't put the gun down, the police will be nervous when they come."

He put it down softly. "I probably shouldn't have picked it up."

"What happened?"

"I heard a gun go off in here when I was coming back from the bathroom. I heard someone running down the hall, but I couldn't see them. I went into the office and found the dead man. I picked up the gun, then you came in."

I hugged myself and rubbed my arms. This wasn't going to look good. "Is that your gun?"

"Yep."

"I thought you kept it locked up."

"I do, but I took it out to clean it. I left it on the desk when I went to the bathroom."

I sank down into the computer chair and ran my hands over my face as I thought. Grandpa might be grumpy, but I never would expect him to shoot someone. Still, he'd been acting a little peculiar lately, and who knew what he would do if he found someone snooping in his office?

"Do you know him?" I asked, gesturing to the body.

"I'm not sure. I can't see his face. Should I roll him over?"

"No!" I yelled. He jumped back. "Sorry. Don't touch anything."

"Right. Evidence."

It felt like hours before sirens wailed into town. I looked at the time. It had to be Troy. It hadn't been long enough for an ambulance.

"Come on," I told Grandpa. "We need to meet them so they can see you're unarmed."

He nodded, and we went to the front doors. Troy was getting out of his truck, and two officers followed, getting out of a patrol car. They all had their guns drawn.

"Sit on the steps," I muttered. "You don't want to look like a threat."

I hurried over to Troy. "He says he was in the bathroom when it happened. He said someone ran off, but he couldn't see them. The body's in the office."

Troy nodded. "Alright. We're going to have to take Walt in for questioning."

I nodded.

Troy had one officer lead Grandpa to the patrol car, and I cringed as they put him in. He didn't look half as concerned as I felt.

Troy and the other officer went inside. I sat on the step and waited. More sirens sounded, and I stood and went over near Troy's truck so I wouldn't be in the way. An ambulance drove up the hill and the paramedics rushed inside.

Right when I was about to go crazy, Troy came out, his eyes searching for me. He spotted me and came over. "I don't see anything. No forced entry, no struggle."

"Nothing was locked," I said, looking at the dirt. "And we know one person obviously came in uninvited." I thought of the dead man. Why was he in Grandpa's office?

"I'm going to have to see what forensics find."

I rubbed my arms. "What do you think happened?"

"I'm not sure."

"I'm worried," I admitted. I usually kept my problems to myself. At least, I had since I ended our friendship. I hadn't had anyone to talk to in years, and now Troy was in front of me and I wanted to spill out my worries.

"Do you think Walt did it?" he asked.

I nodded. "I don't want to believe it, but I can't shake the image of Grandpa holding the gun. Why would someone come into the building, go to my grandpa's office, then get shot by another person who shouldn't be there? It seems too unbelievable."

"Stranger things have happened. Try not to worry. I know that sounds ridiculous, but don't go to the worst-case scenario. I'll figure this out and be in contact."

I nodded. If it were fifteen years ago, he would have hugged me. It wasn't, so he just gave me an awkward smile and walked back to the mortuary.

I didn't know where to go. I figured the morgue was a crime scene now and they wouldn't want me there. Uncle Jerry was in the city—and I should probably call him. The only other place I could think of going was the flower shop. It wasn't open, and it wasn't a good place to relax, but I couldn't stand out here all night.

I couldn't tell you a single thing I passed on the way down. I let myself into the shop and sat on a fold-up chair in the back room. It was too early to go to bed, but too late to find anything around Clover Haven that would be open. I should have brought a book. I could read one on my phone, but I didn't bring my charger, and I didn't want it to die. Not that I could focus on a book right now.

This was going to be a long night. I hoped they would take care of Grandpa. Even if he was guilty, there had to be some type of explanation.

My phone rang, scaring me from my thoughts. "Hello?"

"Neeley? It's Troy. The dead man had a wallet on him. His name was Harrison Nance. Does that mean anything to you?"

My brows came together. "He's a gravedigger. I've never met him, but I make out the paychecks."

"You don't know anything about him?"

"Not really. His brother works with him. That's all I know."

"What's his brother's name?"

"Umm... I want to say Mitchel."

"And you don't know anything else about them?"

"No."

"How long have they worked for Walt?"

"A little less than a year."

There was a pause. "Where are you?"

"At my shop."

"Alright. I'll call you again if I need anything." He sounded tired, and I found myself wondering why. What was his life like now? What stresses did he deal with?

I hung up and looked around. I should probably make myself comfortable. It was going to be a long night.

I couldn't sleep without a blanket, no matter how warm it is, so I went out to my car and grabbed my emergency blanket from the trunk. A barking near my feet made me look down. A small pug gazed up at me and wagged his curly little tail.

Looking down the dirt road, I couldn't see anyone he might belong to. The still of evening was upon us, and it would be strange to see anyone over here. People only came in this direction if they were heading to my shop or the morgue. We were a mile from the main part of town, and there wasn't much on the way.

"Where is your human, handsome?" I asked him.

He tilted his head and looked at me with his big, dark eyes.

"Hmm. I don't think anywhere is open that might help you," I said, my mind racing. I didn't want to leave him outside, but I didn't want to take him in if someone was looking for him. For all I knew, he could take himself home.

"Go home," I said, pointing down the road. There was only one way he could have come from. He rubbed up against my leg like a cat. I sighed. I didn't have time to look for his owner. As soon as I pulled open the shop door, he ran in.

"Make yourself at home," I said sarcastically. "You better not potty on anything."

My phone rang again, and I glanced at the screen. It was Troy again.

"Hello?"

"Hey, I got a hold of Mitchel. He said he thought something was strange because Harrison's door was wide open and his dog was gone. That doesn't make sense, though. Why leave his door open, come to the morgue, and then get shot? I think the door thing is a coincidence."

"Was it a pug?"

"Excuse me?"

"The dog. Was it a pug?"

"Yeah."

"He's with me. He pushed himself into the shop. I was just trying to figure out what to do with him."

"Can you keep him? At least overnight?"

"Sure."

"I'll help you figure out what to do with him tomorrow. I bet Mitchel will take him."

"Sounds good. Anything else?"

"I was actually calling to ask about the gun."

"It's Grandpa's. He said he was cleaning it, but he went to the bathroom." Had I already told him that? I couldn't remember.

"Okay. I should probably drive to Crystal Rock and talk to him."

"You better hurry. He's useless after eight. He's probably already asleep in your office."

"I'm headed over right now. Goodnight."

"Goodnight." I tossed my phone on the counter and looked at the dog. I didn't know what tomorrow would bring. But for now, it was me and the pug, and neither of us would be going anywhere.

Chapter 5

"Neeley?"

I groaned and tried to ignore the voice.

"Neeley? Are you alright?"

I yawned and sat up. Jessa stood above me with a frown taking up most of her face.

"What time is it?" I asked, rubbing my eyes.

"Almost nine. Why are you sleeping on the floor, and why is there a dog running around tearing up tissue paper?"

I got to my feet and stretched. "It was a long night last night."

The back door opened as Roberta came in. Her blue long-sleeved shirt was more wrinkled than the T-shirt I'd slept in.

I went to the front and picked up the little mess maker. Pink and blue shredded tissue paper littered the entire floor.

"What do you think you're doing?" I asked him. He licked his nose and wiggled in my arms, so I opened the door and let him out to do his business.

Jessa raised her brow. "What's going on?"

I stood watching the dog. "Someone was shot last night during book club."

"Oh my," Jessa said, fanning herself with her hand. "Who was it?"

"Harrison Nance. He was one of our gravediggers."

Roberta cringed. "And he got shot? In the same building we were in?"

I nodded. "That's his dog."

Jessa opened the door when he came back. "He's a cutie. Look at his little cinnamon roll of a tail."

"Who cares about that when there might be a murderer running around?" Roberta muttered.

"My grandpa was holding the gun," I said. No use hiding it. In a town this size, word was going to spread like wildfire.

Jessa's eyes narrowed. "It couldn't be Walt. He might be a crotchety old man, but he's not a killer."

"I hope not, but it looks bad—at least from what I saw. Tro—Sheriff McGregor hasn't told me his opinion yet. I should probably go up there and see if he's still around."

"Where's Jerry?"

"I called him before I went to sleep. He stayed at a hotel since the morgue was a crime scene. He'll probably be back this afternoon."

I rubbed my lip and thought. There had to be something I'd missed. Grandpa might look guilty, but what if he wasn't? My mind went to the night before.

"The other night, I thought I heard someone in the attic. I should probably tell the sheriff. I'm going to go up there and see if he's still there."

"I'm coming," Jessa said.

"You can't leave me here alone!" Roberta protested. "Not with a killer on the loose!"

"We can all go," I said. "It's not like anyone's going to come to the shop anyway, and if they do, it will be Billie. She can come back."

We hiked up the hill, slower than I normally went. Roberta and Jessa weren't in the best shape, and I carried the dog. Troy's truck was still parked near the building. The poor guy must've been exhausted.

We entered the building, and I smiled when we spotted Troy sleeping with his head on the front desk. I ignored the urge to push back his hair and scolded myself for the thought. Fifteen years ago, I would have scared him awake, but these were different days.

"Should we leave him?" Jessa whispered. "He's probably been awake most of the night."

The dog barked, and Troy jerked up. He rubbed his eyes and looked at us. "Was I asleep? What time is it?"

"Just after nine," I said. "I thought of something. The other night, I heard footsteps in the attic."

He frowned. "And you didn't call the police?"

Jessa snorted. "Don't you know? Neeley doesn't need a man or anyone else's help. She's an independent woman." She winked at me, and I ignored her teasing.

"I had a baseball bat," I said.

He gave me a look. "You should have called."

"I convinced myself it was my imagination."

"Did you check?"

"I can't get into the attic myself, but I went outside and looked to see if any lights were on up there. It was dark. I went back to bed and didn't hear anything else."

"I want to look up there."

"Let's go." We all clomped up the stairs and over to the attic.

"Still no good way up?" he asked.

I shook my head.

"Okay. Ready?"

"Yep." I handed the dog to Jessa and kicked off my shoes.

Troy squatted down, and I climbed onto his shoulders. He took my hands and stood up slowly. I ducked slightly so I wouldn't hit my head and pushed at the small square trapdoor. I pushed it out of the way, blinking away the dust that fell on me.

"Be careful," he said.

He went onto his toes and my head and shoulders went up into the attic. I put my hands on the attic floor and pushed up. Troy grabbed one of my legs and helped me move my foot onto his shoulder. This wasn't as easy as it used to be.

As soon as my foot felt secure, I pushed up gently and pulled myself into the attic. I pushed some rocks over to the side. I'd forgotten I had my middle school rock collection up here. I should have at least organized them.

"Were the two of you acrobats in a former life?" Jessa asked. "You did that like you've done it a hundred times."

In reality, we probably had done it over a hundred times. Of course, I'd been younger back then. I grabbed the ladder we'd smuggled up here so many years ago and lowered it down. Troy took the bottom and guided it to the floor, then opened it.

"There's no way I'm getting my big fanny through there," Roberta said. "I'll wait down here."

"Me too," Jessa said. "We'll guard the ladder."

I looked around the attic, and memories hit me like a freight train. I'd loved this place.

Troy climbed in, too. "Does the light still work?"

"I don't know." I walked over to the wall. There was enough light from the windows to see, but maybe not find clues. "I haven't been up here in fifteen years." I flipped on the light and the room lit up.

"You never came back?"

"I didn't have anyone to throw me up here."

He nodded and scanned the room. "It's dusty."

"Look." I pointed. "The dust is disturbed over here."

Troy walked carefully over and glanced at the ground. "Whoever was up here was wearing socks."

A shiver went down my spine. "That means there was someone here."

"Could it have been Walt or Jerry?"

I shook my head. "No way. They couldn't get up here."

"What if they had a ladder?"

"I still doubt it. Besides, look. There are no prints in the dust where we came in except ours."

His eyes narrowed. "They came in another way. We spent a lot of time up here. If there was another way out, don't you think we would have found it?"

"I would think so." I tried to ignore the three camp chairs and the dusty board game that had never been put away. There was a lot of stuff up here we had left... since we'd planned to come back.

"Wow. It looks like we didn't finish that game," Troy said, following my gaze. "Hey, and look. It's my college science paper. I had to redo that."

I ignored the guilt. It was my fault he never got to come back up here.

"Stay here," he said. "I'm going to see what's been disturbed."

I nodded and leaned over to pick up a beaded bracelet I'd made in middle school. I shoved it in my pocket. Troy's old green high school hoodie sat on one of the camp chairs. He'd worn it all the time.

Troy disappeared into one of the small spiral staircases. I wanted to follow him. I hadn't been up in the towers for so long. Instead, I grabbed his hoodie and shook the dust off of it. I coughed and looked around guiltily. Approaching the entrance, I dropped to my hands and knees, peering through.

"Roberta? Will you throw this in my room?" I tossed the hoodie down.

"Sure thing." She grabbed it and disappeared down the hall. I stood back up and fanned my hot face. I'd just stolen Troy's hoodie and for what? Because I was crazy. That was the only thing I could think of. I needed fewer reminders of Troy, not more.

I crossed my arms and waited. Troy was sure taking his sweet time.

"Neeley?" he called.

"Yeah?"

"Come up here. Try not to touch anything."

I made my way to the tower stairs, stepping carefully to avoid prints. The narrow steps were as awkward as ever. When I reached the top, sunlight blinded me until I squinted past it.

Troy stood near a small square hole in the floor. "Look what I found," he said, pointing down. "It was hidden under the carpet."

I looked into the hole. A metal ladder descended into darkness. I couldn't see the bottom.

"How did we never find this?" My brows drew together. "Where do you suppose it goes?"

Troy pulled out a flashlight, grinning. "Let's find out."

He disappeared down the ladder. I followed, heart racing.

"It's a closet," he said as I reached the bottom.

Light leaked through a doorframe. I pushed it open—and froze.

"This is Jerry's room."

"Why would he have a ladder going up to the attic?"

I shrugged. "I don't know how I never knew about this. I've only been in this room a few times. He has to know it's here. It's in his closet."

"Jerry might go up into the attic sometimes and you heard him."

I shook my head in denial. "No. I told him I'd heard something up there. He didn't say a word."

"Hmm. Let's go back up."

We climbed back into the tower and left everything the way we found it. Back in the attic, I inspected the space a little closer.

I pointed. "The footprints go over to those boxes by the wall." Ten boxes lined the back wall, and there were so many footprints it was just a mess stirred around in the dust.

"Were those boxes here when we used to come up?"

"I can't remember."

"Neither can I." He lifted the lid off the top box. "No dust. And whoa. This looks valuable."

I hurried over and looked in. "Wow." Jewelry twinkled up at me. A big ruby brooch caught my eye. "Do you think it's real?"

"Probably. Why else hide it up here?"

"Do you think it's connected to the murder?"

"It's possible." He rubbed his temples. "I wish I wasn't so tired. My eyes don't want to focus."

"Did you talk to my grandpa?"

"Yeah."

I fidgeted. "And?"

He sighed, and his eyes locked on mine. "I think he did it."

My mouth turned down. "Oh."

"I don't think he'll get in trouble. My bet is that Harrison came into his office and scared him or something. I think it was an accident."

I nodded. "Now what?"

"We're going to have to keep him for a couple of days. I'm going to have to block off the mortuary as well. I don't want people coming in or out until I can look at all this stuff. Something shady must have been going on, or maybe Jerry has a side hustle. It's hard to know."

"Does that mean I have to keep sleeping at the flower shop?"

"No. You can stay here. Not Jerry, though. Not until I have a long talk with him. I might have to take a nap first, though. I'm not at my best. I'll just sleep in my truck for an hour or two."

"That's ridiculous. We have three guest rooms. You can stay here. That will make it easier for you."

He nodded, appearing grateful. "I'm going to make a few calls, then I'll take you up on that."

"Can I go talk to my grandpa?"

"Yes. I'll call and let them know you're coming."

"Thanks."

Troy walked over to the camp chairs. "Dang. I thought I saw my old hoodie when I came up here. I must have been seeing things. I lost it a long time ago. I loved that thing."

I pursed my lips and felt the temperature in my face rise a few degrees. What had I been thinking?

"Let's go," I said, moving toward the exit. I put my feet through and found the ladder. I climbed down, then closed the ladder and lifted it up. Troy grabbed it and pulled it through the opening. A few moments later, he lowered himself down, then dropped to the floor.

"That was an amazing drop," Jessa said. "I see why you're the sheriff."

Troy grinned. "What, because I'm crazy?"

Jessa laughed. "That helps sometimes."

"Find anything?" Roberta asked.

"Maybe," Troy said. "We won't know for a while."

Normally at this point, I would have climbed back on Troy's shoulders and closed the attic, but if Troy would be coming and going, it didn't really matter. It also occurred to me that we could come and go from Jerry's room if we wanted to.

"I'll go up through Jerry's room next time," he said, as if he had read my mind. "When I'm up there, I'll close this."

"Sounds good."

Jessa handed me the dog, and I rubbed his ears. I needed to go visit my grandpa, but that would have to wait. This little guy needed breakfast.

Chapter 6

I walked through the small trailer park that Mitchel Nance lived in and looked at the numbers on the trailers. The area was well-kept and not what I'd expected. I had the pug under one arm, and a plate of cookies in the other.

When I found the right place, I used my elbow to ring the doorbell. The door opened a crack, and a man peeked out.

"What?" he asked.

"I'm Neeley Kelter. Walt's granddaughter? I have Harrison's dog."

The door opened the rest of the way, and a middle-aged man in overalls glared out at me. He was balding on top and had brown hair on the sides. His arms looked strong, which made sense if he dug graves. Most people used machinery to dig these days, but Grandpa insisted doing it with shovels was better. He had no good logic, just a stubborn streak.

The dog growled at the man.

"I'm not taking Murphy," he said. "He's not my responsibility."

I handed him the cookies. "I'm sorry about your loss."

He nodded and pulled the cling wrap from the plate. "You should be, since it sounds like your grandpa did it." He took a cookie from the plate and shoved it into his mouth.

I rubbed my lips together. "Is there anything I can do?"

"Just keep people away from me. And Murphy. I don't have the time or patience for a dog. I assume I still have a job?"

"Yes, of course."

"Great." He shut the door, and I stood staring at it.

I glanced down at Murphy. "Nice guy."

Murphy cuddled into me, and I held him close. "It looks like you and I are going to be roommates, Murph. Can I call you Murph?"

His tongue drooped out of his mouth, which I interpreted as yes.

I drove back to the flower shop and asked Jessa to look after Murphy, then I made my way toward Crystal Rock and the police station. I would have to stop at McKenzie's grocery store to pick up some dog supplies. McKenzie's was overpriced, but nothing like the thirteen dollars I'd spent earlier today to get three cups' worth of dry dog food at the Clover Haven store.

With luck, McKenzie didn't still work there. She'd been a nightmare in high school. She'd drooled over Troy and Chase worse than almost anyone, and I'd managed to avoid her for the most part.

I pulled into the police station and went into the red brick building. A woman at the front called an officer and had him take me back to my grandpa.

I frowned when I saw him sitting in a cell on a small bed. He looked up from a magazine he was reading.

"Neeley, what are you doing here?" he asked, turning a page.

"I'm checking on you. I didn't think they would put you in a cell."

"It's comfy. I've been catching up on my reading. Food's good too."

Grandpa was a complainer, so his attitude surprised me.

I took the bars between my hands and looked in. "Did you know there was a ladder in Uncle Jerry's room that goes up to the attic?"

He chuckled. "I sure do. We used to laugh at the lengths you kids would go through to get up there."

My eyes narrowed. "You knew we went up there?"

"Sure did. You made a lot of racket."

I blinked. We'd thought we were so clever.

He yawned. "You haven't been up there in a while."

"I went up today."

"I bet it's dusty."

I nodded. I wouldn't say anything. I wasn't sure what information Troy wanted getting around, especially to the number one suspect.

"I'm going to get you out of here," I promised.

"No hurry. It's made me realize how nice it might be to retire. I never thought I would, but it might be close to time. Jerry would like that."

"Why?"

"He's always wanted to run the place."

"I didn't know that."

"He tried to buy me out a few times."

"Interesting."

He raised his brow. "Don't get that look. You know your uncle isn't behind any of this."

"But if you went to jail, he would take over?"

"Yes. I promised he could have it if anything ever happened to me. You don't have to worry. He said he would take care of you, and you get it when he dies."

"I don't need to be taken care of."

"I suppose that's true. Your parents left you set for life. Still, family is important. He'll be there for you."

"That's your time," the officer standing behind me said.

I nodded. "Bye, Grandpa. I love you."

"Yep," he said.

Grandpa had always taken care of me, but he wasn't an overly affectionate person. I wasn't sure if he'd ever told me he loved me except in cards he gave me for my birthday.

Sometimes I wondered if that was why Troy, Chase, and I were so tight. We all needed each other. Troy's parents were bossy and always off doing things, and Chase was raised by his aunt. She was fun and loved all of us, so we gravitated to her. I'd missed her since I'd ruined the friendship.

I drove over to McKenzie's and entered the store with a mission to be in and out in five minutes. The store only had a few aisles, and I hoped one carried pet supplies. If not, I was in for a longer drive.

I smiled when I saw a small section of dog food, as well as dishes and a few other odds and ends. I filled my arms and walked up to the register. I scowled when I saw McKenzie and her bleached ponytail ready to check me out.

"Neeley Kelter! Is that you?" McKenzie squealed like we'd been long-lost friends.

I gave her a half smile. "Yep."

"I haven't seen you in ages."

I placed my things on the conveyor belt and remembered why I drove the extra time to the city.

"How are things in Clover Haven?" she asked, scanning a leash.

"Fine." Short answers were safe.

"I thought you were avoiding Crystal Rock."

"I try."

She laughed. "I bet."

I didn't know what she meant by that, and I didn't want to.

"Have you seen Troy or Chase lately?" she pried.

"I talked to Troy today."

She smiled, and I realized that, even at thirty-five, I wasn't old enough to forgive the past. I still wanted to roll my eyes every time she opened her mouth.

"That's amazing! You all used to be such good friends. It's a pity you had that little spat."

What did she know about it?

I smiled. "And it's a pity you don't have a self-checkout."

Her smile waned for a moment and came back. "Did you know I'm dating someone?"

Some people never change. "Nope. I don't care what happens in Crystal Rock." I knew I was being a jerk, but McKenzie had always been rude when we were younger. Not that it excused me.

"He's adorable," she said, ignoring my comment. "He helps me run the store. It's nice to have a smart guy around. What about you? Are you dating anyone?"

"Nope."

"Really? I could set you up with someone."

I shook my head. "Nope."

"And it looks like you have a dog now..."

I put my debit card in the reader, punched in some numbers, and grabbed my bag. "See you."

"Bye!" She waved. "Don't be a stranger."

I hurried out to my car and jumped in. I didn't need to have any more reunions from my past. McKenzie always pretended to be nice, while insulting a person at the same time. I spent most of the ride thinking about all the times McKenzie had embarrassed or annoyed me in the past, and by the time I got back to the flower shop, I'd worked myself up into a terrible mood.

It didn't help when I went in and saw Billie.

She turned and glared at me. "There is a dog in here."

"I know."

"Jessa said he's yours?"

"He is."

"What if people are allergic?"

I shrugged. "I don't have a good place to keep him right now."

"Yes, I heard about Walt. Pity. And to think. I was in the mortuary when it happened."

"We don't know what happened yet, so it would be good to not speculate until we do."

"Do you have any tulips?"

"No. Tulips are hard to keep, and this isn't the best time of year to get them."

"Fine. Give me a bouquet of something with the main color purple."

I ground my teeth, and Jessa must have sensed my mood. "I'll make one for you," she said.

I reached down and grabbed Murphy. "I'm taking him up to the mortuary." I grabbed the dog supplies from the trunk and walked up the hill. Murphy licked my face, and I wasn't sure whether to be disgusted or enchanted. I felt a little of both.

When I got to the doors, Uncle Jerry came rushing out with a backpack over his shoulder, ducking under the crime scene tape. As far as I knew, I was the only person besides the police who was allowed to go in.

"What are you doing?" I asked.

"Just grabbing some clothes," he said. "If I have to stay at a hotel, I don't want to buy a new wardrobe."

I supposed that made sense. I went inside and up to my room. Grandpa wouldn't want a dog running all over the place, so he was going to have to spend most of his time in my room. I might be able to block the stairs so he could run around the third floor.

I put Murphy down on my light brown carpet, and he began exploring the place. Then I placed the small dog bed I'd gotten in the corner and his dishes next to it.

A knock on the door almost made my heart stop. I'd thought I was the only one here. We didn't normally lock the front door, so it wasn't unheard of to have people wander in.

"Yes?"

"It's Troy. Can I come in?"

I grabbed his hoodie from the top of my clean laundry pile and shoved it under my mattress, then I hurried to the door and opened it.

"Hey." I wondered how guilty I looked.

"Hi. I've been down at the cemetery, and I was wondering what's happening there?"

I gave him a half-smile. "Not much. It's usually pretty dead."

His mouth twitched. "It looks like someone has been doing something to some of the graves? Digging by them."

My eyes narrowed. "New graves?"

"No. They're pretty old."

I moved my jaw from side to side. "Let me go look with you."

He nodded and stepped to the side.

I glanced at Murphy. "I might have to take the dog. I'm not sure how well he'll do at not making a mess." I grabbed the new leash and ripped off the tags, then clipped it to Murphy's collar.

The dog ran in circles as I tried to get him to go straight.

Troy laughed. "Calm down, buddy."

He took off out the door, and I hurried over and picked him up. I wasn't sure how he would do on the stairs with his pudgy little legs. When we got out, I put him back down, and with some prodding, he went in the right direction.

The cemetery was on the other side of the hill, behind the morgue. It wasn't huge, but it'd been around for a long time, so it wasn't small either. We walked down a dirt road, and Murphy charged ahead faster than I wanted. If I tried to pull back, he would whine.

"Are you keeping the dog?" Troy asked.

"Yes. Mitchel doesn't want him."

"What does Walt think about that?"

"He doesn't know yet."

We walked through some weeds, then over to the grass surrounding the graves. Troy led me over to some old gravestones, and I chewed my lip when I looked at the overturned dirt in front of them. The area that was disturbed was big enough to have unearthed an entire coffin.

"It looks like someone dug here," I said. "Grave robbers maybe?"

Troy's eyes scanned the area. "It's hard to say."

"We ask people not to bury valuables, but in the end, we don't police them. I rarely see anything get buried that's worth anything, so I think it would be a waste of someone's time. And would grave robbers rebury them? I would think they would want to get in and out fast."

"That's what I would think. I'm probably going to have to dig some of them up to see if anything has been disturbed. I wonder about those boxes full of things in the attic."

"You think it's stuff from the graves?"

"I'm not sure, but it might be."

I pressed my lips into a line. "I don't think it's legal to start digging up graves. Even for the sheriff."

"I have to talk to a judge. I don't think it will be a problem. You usually have to get permission from the closest family members, but these are too old for that to matter."

"How long will that take?"

"Hopefully no more than a few days. I've already got things rolling. I think I'll need someone from the mortuary to be here to supervise."

"I suppose I can do that. Or Jerry."

"Do you trust him?"

I shrugged. "I'm not sure. He was at the morgue today. He said he was getting clothes."

Troy sighed. "I told him he couldn't come unless someone was with him."

I walked around, looking at the graves. "The ones with the disturbed earth, they all have the same last name."

Troy examined them all. "Brightman. I'm not sure if that is significant or not."

"Do you know that name?" I turned to Troy.

He shook his head.

I stared at the earth. "Then I guess we're not just dealing with a murder. Someone's digging up the past—literally."

Chapter 7

"Sheriff McGregor is joining us today," I told the book club a few days later. Troy said we could hold the book club, but he had to be there, and no one could leave the room without an escort.

Troy sat at the table and gave a small wave.

"Glad to have you," Billie said. "You should join us every time. We need more men's opinions."

"That would be nice," Jim agreed. "I get drowned out most of the time."

"You talk plenty."

Jim laughed. "Not as much as you."

Billie glared at him. "And there's good reason we don't want to hear from you."

I passed around a plate of cookies. I'd forgotten to assign someone to make dessert, so I'd ended up throwing something together. Thankfully, cookies were something I was good at. I'd perfected this recipe in high school, and people around here always requested my cookies.

Troy took a bite and smiled. "It's been a while."

Troy and Chase had been my taste testers as I perfected the recipe, and had helped me eat all the experiments.

"I loved the book," Lydia said. "I even had a dream about it. That's how much I was thinking about it."

"There was no kissing," Jessa said. "Minus one point."

"It will get there," Roberta told her. "Probably in book two or three."

"Yeah, but we read so many books that I never have time to read anything but the assigned book. I've read tons of book ones and no book twos."

"Why don't we read book two next, then?" I suggested. It wasn't an issue for me. I read a book a night sometimes, so if I liked the series, I usually finished it.

"Good idea," Jessa said. "I'm for that."

"I don't understand why you all want romance in your mysteries," Jim said. "What's the point?"

"I vote we ignore Jim," Billie said. "What did you think of the book, Sheriff?"

Troy swallowed his cookie. "It was alright."

"You read it?" I asked in surprise.

"I read it while I was sitting with nothing to do at the courthouse."

"And it was only 'alright?'" Lydia tilted her head. "I thought it was great."

"It's not my genre. There was nothing wrong with it."

"Need something a bit grittier?" Billie asked. "I suppose being the sheriff might make you that way."

"No, I prefer more mild stuff. I don't want to think about work when I'm reading. I don't actually read much. Things are busy."

"This is a small town. How busy could they be?"

"There's been a lot going on in Crystal Rock lately. It's been hard to keep up with."

"Any ideas about who killed Harrison?" Jim asked.

Troy shrugged. "I'm sure it will all come together."

"I thought it would be faster," Viola said. "I can't believe it happened while we were all here."

"You were in the bathroom, though, weren't you?" Billie asked.

Viola frowned. "Yes, but I was still in the morgue."

"You could have been shooting Harrison."

Viola threw her head back and laughed. "And why would I do that? I'd never met the man."

"I'm just saying... someone was shot, and you weren't accounted for."

"Let's talk about the book," I suggested. "And eat more cookies."

"Yes," Viola said, "there's nothing better than books and cookies." Viola was the only member of the group close to my age. She dressed up every time, just like Billie. Today she had a long evening dress and gloves that went up to her elbows.

"Of course she wants to change the subject," Billie muttered. "Since she looks guilty."

"Goodness, Billie," Viola said. "I went to the bathroom, heard the gun, and hurried back here. Why would I shoot someone I don't know?"

"Maybe you did know him."

"I'm not talking to you, Billie."

I hoped the night would get better, but it didn't. It was one fight after another. By the time book club was over, I was ready to fall into bed. I had too much to do, though. I still needed to figure out what had happened so I could clear my grandpa's name. Ever since I saw the turned dirt at the graves, I was almost sure someone else was guilty.

After everyone left, I went up to my room and fed Murphy, then got ready for bed. I pulled Troy's hoodie over my nightshirt and climbed into the sheets with my laptop. I wasn't sure why I'd taken the hoodie—or why I was wearing it. After all these years of trying to forget Troy, this wasn't helping.

I opened my computer and pulled out a paper that I'd copied all the names from the headstones on. There had to be some sort of connection besides having the same last name.

I was almost sure my search would be pointless, but the first name and birthdate I put in brought up several results. I clicked on the first one.

Tennison Brightman had lived in Clover Haven when it was founded. He'd struck it rich while mining gold. I clicked on another site that listed his family tree. All the names on the tombs were closely related to him.

Murphy finished his dinner and ran toward my bed. He jumped, missed the top of the mattress by a few inches, and fell back, rolling on the floor.

"Too high?" I asked with a chuckle. I scooped him up and let him sit on the bed.

I clicked on another link and read everything I could about Tennison Brightman. When I was done, Murphy was fast asleep at the foot of my bed. I would let him stay this time, but tomorrow I'd get him to sleep in his bed.

Curling up, I pulled my legs into the hoodie and my blanket up to my chin and thought about all the things I'd read. Tennison had been worth a lot. When he died, his kids had fought over his fortune. Some of it was unaccounted for, and people assumed it was stolen.

All of his children had ended up with small fortunes, and a lot of it had disappeared after their deaths. There was a lot of speculation and people searching for the wealth, but it had never been found.

What if all the stuff in the attic boxes was what everyone had been looking for? I assumed Troy had taken it all and would find out whether it was real and what it was worth. After twenty minutes of not being able to sleep, I decided to go to the attic to see if he'd taken it.

I hurried out of my room and into Uncle Jerry's. I couldn't believe I'd never known about the attic access in here. I would have been up there more. Reading in the towers would be majestic. I'd never done it because I couldn't get up without help. It might become something I would begin once everything settled.

I climbed up the ladder, pushed on the trapdoor at the top, and climbed up. Descending the stairs and entering the attic, I was cautious not to touch a thing. To my disappointment, when I switched on the lights, all the boxes were gone, taken by Troy.

A movement at my left made me freeze.

Someone was up here.

My heart raced as my palms grew damp.

They'd gone behind the wall to the stairs on the opposite tower from where I'd come. I had two choices. I could go see who it was, or I could get out of here as fast as I could. My feet didn't seem to want to do either.

Troy was in a guest room. I could call him. Then he would find me frozen here in his hoodie. I shook my head. Alternatively, he'd find me dead in his hoodie, all because I didn't want him to know I took it.

Something glittered on the floor, and I bent to pick it up. I didn't have time to analyze it, so I stuck it in my pocket.

Whoever was here wasn't moving, and neither was I.

I kept my eyes fixed on the place they had disappeared. They couldn't leave without coming out. Why hadn't I taken my baseball bat with me?

The biggest thing I could see was a camp chair. I took it and folded it up. It was the best weapon I could come up with. I tiptoed to the place I was sure the person had gone, and I jumped around the corner, the chair held like a bat.

No one was there.

Now I felt stupid, but at least no one had seen me. I walked up the steps, knowing they had to be at the top of the tower.

When I got to the top, I frowned. Someone had pulled back the carpet, just like on the other side, and there was another trap door.

"Are you kidding me?" I muttered.

I uncovered the trapdoor and climbed down the ladder. This was crazy. I was following someone who might be a murderer. In my head, I was almost convinced it was my uncle. Who else could know about these passages? I got to the ground and pushed open a closet. I walked into a dark room, and my stomach dropped. The person could be hiding anywhere, and I didn't know which room I was in.

I took a few steps into the dark, the chair clutched in my hands. I hoped whoever was here was as unable to see as I was.

A light clicked on, and I squealed and turned toward it, the chair ready to swing.

Troy sat up in bed, the lamp by his nightstand on. "Neeley? What are you doing?"

I took a deep breath and spun around, scanning the room. I couldn't see anyone. "Someone's in here." I lowered the chair slowly.

"It's me."

"No. There's another attic access in your closet. Didn't you look in there?"

"No." He sounded ruffled. "I only have a few changes of clothes, so I left them in my bag."

"I went up to the attic, and someone was there. They came this way, didn't you hear them?"

"I just woke up a minute ago when I heard the closet close and you breathing hard."

"They could still be here."

I looked at the gun on his lap. "Why is your gun out?"

"I didn't know who was in the room." He stood up and looked around. "There aren't a lot of places to hide in here." He moved the curtains and looked under the bed. "If I was asleep, they probably got out. How did we not know about these ways to the attic? We were all over this place when we were young."

"This was my aunt's room. We never came in here or in Jerry's room. I don't think my grandpa wanted us to know how easy it was to get up there."

"I better go look outside," he said, grabbing my hand and pulling me with him. "I don't want you wandering around alone."

It was the first time I'd felt his hand in mine for so long. I tried not to think too much about it, tried not to concentrate on the speed of my heart.

We went downstairs and into the lobby. The front door was wide open.

"Whoever it is, is gone," he said. "What's with the chair?"

"It's a weapon."

"I see...." His eyes sparkled. "Hey. Is that my hoodie?"

I looked at the green hoodie, then up at him. "What are you talking about? Everyone at our school had these hoodies."

"And you've been wearing it for all these years?"

"I guess they're durable."

"I never saw you wear one."

"Maybe you didn't pay attention."

He rubbed his chin and gave me a look I couldn't interpret. "I paid attention. I can't believe you're wearing it after all these years."

"I can't believe you're wearing Scooby Doo pajama bottoms."

He grinned. "I hope you aren't going to spread that around."

I smirked. "I'll think about it. It's kind of funny to think about the sheriff running around with a gun and those pants."

Troy's smile faded. "I know it looks like the person left, but I better check the entire place to be safe."

I nodded. Troy knew this place as well as I did.

"I'll check your room first, then you can lock yourself inside."

I sighed as he walked me up to my room. I couldn't fall back into our old routine, but I already was. We'd always teased each other, and that was part of what I loved about Troy.

He checked anywhere a person could hide in my room, and I put the chair against the wall. I hoped I wouldn't be needing it.

He glanced at me. "You let the dog sleep in your bed?"

"Only tonight."

He smirked. "That's what they all say."

"I was tired tonight, so I didn't want to deal with it." I reached into the pocket of the hoodie and pulled out whatever it was I'd found in the attic. "I found this." I handed it to him.

"What is it?"

I looked closer. It was thin and had five gems surrounded by a gold frame. There was a place for two more stones, but they were missing. "I dunno. A hair decoration or something like that."

"I'll put it with the other stuff."

"Where is that?"

"I have a guy checking it all to see what it's worth."

"Is it all real?"

"It seems to be."

"I wonder if it was all in graves and someone knew, or at least suspected."

He looked behind my long drapes. "Possibly. It's clear. Make sure you lock the door when I leave and call me if you hear anything strange."

"Okay."

He left, and I locked the door. I flipped off the light and walked to the bed, trying not to think about how dark it was. I made sure I didn't bump Murphy and climbed under the blanket. I wasn't sure what scared me more: someone sneaking through the house, or how safe I felt with Troy just one door away.

Chapter 8

The flower shop was a disaster. I stood in the middle of the store and clenched and unclenched my teeth. Whoever did this didn't just want to cause trouble—they wanted to destroy something beautiful. The petals weren't just scattered, they were shredded. Even the stems were sliced into neat, malicious little pieces.

The door opened, and Jessa came in. "Whoa!" she exclaimed, glancing around. "This is a mess! Who would do something like this?"

"I don't know," I said, looking around. "It's going to take forever to clean." It was my guess that whoever had been at the morgue last night had run down the hill and to the shop. I couldn't see a good reason for anyone to do this.

"Did you call the police?"

"No. I just got here. I'm not sure we should bother Sheriff McGregor. He was up most of the night."

"Oh, yeah?"

"Someone was in the morgue."

"Did he catch them?"

"No. I bet they came here right after."

Jessa rubbed a braid between her fingers. "It must have taken forever. It looks like they even cut up the fake flowers."

"Perhaps they wanted to take some attention off of other things." I went into the back and checked the locked coolers. I sighed with relief when I saw they were untouched. Everything in there was being picked up today. "They didn't touch the Smiths' flowers."

"That's good. I bet breaking those locks would have been too much effort." Jessa gave me a pointed look. "You need to call the sheriff. We can't clean up until he looks around."

My nose wrinkled. "I suppose you're right." Troy didn't answer, so I hung up when it went to voicemail. "I might have to go wake him."

"Go ahead."

"I don't want to leave you here alone. I'll wait until Roberta comes." My phone rang. "Never mind, that's him. Hello?"

"Sorry I missed the call. What's wrong?"

"Someone was in the flower shop. They made a mess."

"I'll be down in a minute."

I hung up and went to check the doors to make sure they weren't ruined. I was crazy about locking up, so I knew I did it. I always checked two or three times just to be sure. Jessa teased me for being paranoid.

"No marks by the door," I said, running my hand over the unbothered wood.

"I've been thinking," Jessa said nonchalantly. "It was a little crazy the other day when the sheriff boosted you up into the attic. He didn't give you instructions, you just climbed right on his shoulders. It was like the two of you had been rehearsing."

I took a deep breath. The flower shop was in ruins and she wanted to talk about that.

Roberta smiled as she entered from the back. "I was actually thinking the same thing when it happened. It was like you'd done it a hundred times."

I crossed my arms and glared at both of them. "We have done it a hundred times."

Jessa raised her eyebrow. "Why? That seems like a random thing to do with the sheriff whom you seem to hate."

I rubbed my arms. "About a million years ago, I had a group of friends. We liked to study and play games in the attic. Grandpa didn't like us up there, so we had to come up with a way to get up without him knowing."

"And the sheriff was one of those friends?"

"Yeah."

"And now you avoid him. Why is that?"

"It doesn't matter. He just bugs me," I lied. "I think I'm getting used to him again. I can be civil."

"That's good." Jessa nodded. "I wouldn't want him avoiding us to get away from you. It's good to have someone fabulous to stare at every once in a while."

"Amen to that." Roberta snickered.

I shook my head and held in a smile. "You two are ridiculous."

Jessa grinned. "You wouldn't be saying that if you'd seen the sheriff's biceps when he was pushing you up into the attic."

I gave a half smile. "He's always had nice arms."

The door opened, and Troy stepped in. "Who are we talking about? Whoa, they really did a number in here." Troy's eyes swept the room like he was memorizing it. He didn't ask more about the arms comment, thank goodness.

"I don't think anything is permanently damaged, besides the flowers."

"This is my fault," he said, walking around, scanning the floor. "Last night I should have looked around the outside better."

"I'm sure it took long enough searching the entire morgue."

He pulled out his phone and sent a text. "I'm going to have another officer or two come if they can. We're spread a little thin these days. Is there anything in the back room?"

"No. They might have taken flowers out of there, but the mess is all here."

Roberta tripped over a chair and stabilized herself. Sometimes it shocked me she didn't have more injuries.

"Were the doors locked?"

Jessa laughed. "You better believe it, hon. Neeley is a crazy door locker. I bet she gets up at night sometimes and runs down just to make sure it's locked, even though she already checked three times before she left."

"I've only done that a few times." It happened about once a month, but I wouldn't admit that.

He went to the front window and inspected it. "Who is it that has nice arms?"

I felt the color in my face drain.

Roberta snickered, and Jessa smiled.

I glared at both of them. "Lots of people have nice arms. The guy who plays Thor, for example."

He looked up. "Hmm. I guess so."

"There's no guess. He has nice arms."

Troy chuckled and went to check a side window. "There's scraping near the lock. My guess is they came in here. It's unlocked."

I went over and looked. "I'll have to put something extra on the windows so no one can do that."

"I'll have forensics come by to scan for prints. It might take a while because they aren't close. I'll need you to stay closed."

"I'll grab the flowers from the back. I have people coming for them today."

"I can deliver them," Jessa said. "I need something to do."

"Thanks." I wondered how I could fill the day. I couldn't stay here, and Troy didn't want me wandering around the morgue more than I had to.

"I'll help," Roberta said.

"Take the van."

We had a company minivan that we hardly used. For the most part, it sat on the side of the shop helping advertise.

It took a few minutes to load the flowers into the van. Then I waved as Jessa and Roberta rode off.

I stepped back into the shop and found Troy. "Hey, I figured some stuff out last night when I searched for information about the Brightman family. I can show you if I go grab my laptop."

"There's not a lot I can do here until I get more people. I'll come with you and you can show me."

We went up to the morgue and sat on my bed while I pulled up my saved searches from the night before. I showed him the story about Tennison Brightman, and then the family chart.

Murphy jumped up on my legs, and when I didn't pick him up, he jumped on Troy. Troy absentmindedly picked him up.

He squinted as he studied the computer. "All the people whose graves were dug up... they were Tennison Brightman's children?"

"That's what it looks like."

He scrolled down through the family tree. "Isn't that interesting?"

"What?" I asked, scanning the screen.

"Down here." He pointed at a name. Jeff Nance.

My eyes went wide. "Nance? Do you think Harrison and Mitchel are related to the Brightmans?"

"That's my guess. Nance isn't a common name. At least as far as I know."

"Did they know there was stuff buried with their ancestors? Maybe that's why the graves are dug up."

"Could be. I should have found this. There's never enough time to do all the things that need doing."

"I know our county has a lot of small towns, but couldn't they hire more officers?"

He scratched the stubble on his jaw. "We're usually fine. Things have been more hectic lately, but I'm hoping it calms down."

Murphy licked Troy's face, and he flinched.

I smiled. "I didn't think dog slobber would faze you."

"Most things dogs do I can ignore. Not licking my face."

Troy had always had dogs growing up, and his patience with them had always impressed me.

"Murphy is a cuddler. He might be getting tired of hanging out in my room. There isn't a lot to do."

"Do you trust me?"

I wrinkled my nose. "What do you mean?"

"I need to go look around the outside of your shop. I can take him with me."

"Oh. Sure. I bet he would love that."

I went to my dresser and grabbed the leash from the top and handed it to him. Once they left, I paced around my room. I needed to do something. Grandpa might be enjoying his prison stunt, but I wanted him safe and home.

Twenty minutes later, I found myself in front of Mitchel's trailer. I knocked and waited.

He opened the door and sighed. "You again?"

"Can I ask you a few questions?"

"I suppose, but only because you made me cookies last time. Come in."

I didn't mention that he should be nice to the person who signs his paycheck. I entered the trailer and looked around in shock. It was nicer than a lot of homes I'd been in, and it didn't feel squished like I'd always imagined.

"Sit." He motioned at a gray leather sofa. I sat and wondered if I should have brought pepper spray. He sat in a chair across from me and crossed his arms. "What do you want?"

"I'm wondering about your brother."

He scratched his nose. "I'm getting tired of talking about him. The sheriff's been here a bunch and a few other officers."

"Do you have any ideas about what happened to Harrison?"

"Harrison was an idiot. I can imagine lots of people wanted to kill him."

I blinked. Not what I expected. "Oh?"

"He begged me to come. I don't usually take jobs that involve digging by hand. Who even does that anymore?"

"My grandpa is a little particular."

"I did it because the money was good."

"It's okay, but I wouldn't say good."

"Harrison was paying me more than my salary."

"He must have really wanted you to be here."

He grumbled. "Which means he was up to something. That's how he was. I didn't ask, I just came."

"We think some graves have been tampered with. Graves of people you are related to."

His eyes narrowed. "People I'm related to?"

"Yes. The Brightmans."

He leaned back. "I'm confused."

"There is the possibility that someone has been robbing graves."

He looked to the side and tapped his fingers on his knee. "I bet... no... maybe.... Hmm."

I waited for him to work out his thoughts.

He glanced at me. "The Brightmans were wealthy, but it was said they never had as much money as they should. My grandma said the rumor was that they had a lot of their wealth buried with them. Only the family knew, because they didn't want to deal with grave robbers. Dang it. That's what this is all about."

I leaned forward. "What?"

"I couldn't figure out why Harrison wanted me to work here so bad. He made me do most of the graves while he slept. I bet he was digging up the graves at night. He wanted to be rested so he could dig at night. I didn't pay him any attention. I figured he was just lazy. I bet Tori's in on it."

"Tori?"

"My sister. She does whatever ridiculous thing Harrison comes up with. She was here a few times over the last month or so."

"Did Harrison live with you?"

"No. He had another trailer. This seems to be the only place in town to rent anything and not have to sign a long-term contract. I wasn't going to stay with him. He might cause damage that I don't want to pay for. Harrison wasn't a responsible man. He's been in jail a few times."

"Where is Tori?"

"No clue. I don't have her contact information. We've never been close. I don't even know if she knows about Harrison."

"Are you staying around now?"

"Not for long. The sheriff asked me to stay until the investigation is over. I was going to send in my notice, but with the boss in jail, I don't know where to send it."

"I'll take care of it."

"Great."

A million more questions hovered just out of reach. They'd come to me the second I walked out the door.

Chapter 9

I folded my arms and glared at Troy. "You want me to watch you dig up a grave?"

He stood on the steps of the mortuary, and his mouth turned down. "It's worse than that."

"Oh?"

He pulled off his sunglasses and rubbed his chin. "I need to watch *you* dig up graves."

"Excuse me?"

"I got all the permission and things I need from a judge, but a condition for digging up the graves is that it has to be done by someone who works at the mortuary. Walt is out of the question, and your uncle is avoiding my calls. That leaves you, or the maid."

He grinned slightly, and I frowned.

"As far as the court's concerned, you're still on file as an active employee—even if unpaid."

"Grandpa pays me." I shifted my jaw, calculating just how much dirt I'd have to move. I was in fair shape, but not digging six feet down and eight feet wide kind of shape. "The top of the coffin is four feet down. Are we pulling them all the way out, or opening them while they're down?"

"I'm not sure. We'll have to wing it."

"And how many of these do we need to dig up?"

"Six." He adjusted the backpack on his shoulder.

I stared into Troy's hypnotizing green eyes and raised one eyebrow. "You think I can dig up six graves?"

A glint of amusement flickered in his eyes. "Nope. But I'm out of options, and I'm excited to watch you try."

I tried to keep my face passive, but I was sure my mouth twitched. Troy knew me too well. He knew if he told me I couldn't do something, I was one hundred percent going to do it.

"And you are just going to sit there, staring at me?"

"Yep. It's my job."

I wanted to run down there and have all those graves dug up by evening, but I was also realistic. This was going to kill me.

"What about Mitchel? He still officially works here. Could he help?"

"He's not interested in helping. He said he quit. He was only here to work with Harrison."

I knew not having the correct number of employees was going to bite us someday. This was that day. Why did Grandpa insist on doing so many things by himself?

"Fine. Let's go."

"You might want sunblock."

I nodded and ran inside. I put on sunblock, grabbed a pink floppy sun hat, and my sunglasses. I wasn't sure it went with my jeans and T-shirt, but I wouldn't last without sun protection.

I was back in five minutes with Murphy at my heels.

"Nice hat."

I smiled. "You can borrow it any time."

"I'll remember that."

We went down to the cemetery. Troy had already prepared. There were shovels and water bottles waiting.

I grabbed a shovel and gloves, and went to Tennison Brightman's grave. I put the shovel to the ground and jumped on it. I threw a scoop of dirt to the side, and Troy sat on the grass and opened a water bottle.

"Good job," he said, taking a sip. Murphy wagged his tail and ran in circles.

I smiled. "I lift five-pound weights every day. This will be a cinch."

He grinned. "I remember lifting five-pound weights... in second grade."

I scooped another shovelful of dirt and tossed it on his lap. "Oops. Sorry."

Troy only smiled and brushed it off. This was dangerous territory. If Troy didn't go back to Crystal Rock soon, we were going to become friends again, and I was going to go back to dreaming about what I couldn't have.

I shoveled for a few minutes, and I could already feel pain in my arms. I wasn't stupid, though. I knew Troy. Or I used to. He would give me a few more minutes, and then he would start shoveling, whether it was legal or not.

He lay back, put on his sunglasses, and rested his hands on his stomach. "Nice day."

I thought about throwing another shovelful of dirt onto him, but that would only encourage him.

I dug faster.

He was waiting for me to complain. I wasn't going to.

"There are some nice worms in here," I said, trying to distract myself.

"I bet."

Murphy jumped on his stomach.

"Ooof!" Troy sat up.

I smiled. "Serves you right."

"For what?"

"Being a dork. Get a shovel and start digging."

He laughed and put Murphy on the ground. He stood and took a shovel and gloves and went to the grave next to me.

"I bet I can find a body before you can," he said.

"No way." I picked up speed. We probably sounded morbid, but growing up in a mortuary might have made me less considerate of some things than I should've been.

We dug in silence, and it got to the point that I was forcing myself to keep going. My shoulders were killing, and I was going to have blisters, even with the gloves.

"There's no way Grandpa or Uncle Jerry would have been able to do this, even if they were here." I climbed out of my hole and grabbed a water bottle.

"Probably not."

"What are we hoping to find? If someone dug them up, they probably took anything valuable."

He nodded. "But there might be evidence."

I got back in my hole. This was horrible, and it was probably better than it could have been, because someone had already loosened the dirt. I had to be getting close. At least in this one spot. I was still going to have to go a lot wider.

"Hit it," he said.

I growled. I was probably close. If I hadn't stopped for water, I might have gotten there first. A few more scoops and my shovel hit something.

"I'm not sure I can do this," I admitted.

"We should do one at a time. I'll come over and help you."

Troy came over and we fell into quiet digging.

"You alright?" Troy asked a while later. "You're pale."

I took a deep breath. "I might puke."

"Take a break. Get some water."

I nodded and climbed out of the hole. I sat on the grass and took a swallow from my water bottle. It helped, but my arms were shaking. I wasn't ready for this.

"I feel like if we open the coffin, dirt's going to fall in," Troy said. "I don't see how we could raise it up, though."

I looked in at the dirty coffin and frowned. "This one is all scratched up. I'm sure we could donate new coffins and have them reburied once this is over. These are old enough that the family isn't going to complain."

Troy climbed out of the hole and looked at me. "If you're going to replace them, let's open this one now. We can force it and not worry about the mess falling in."

We'd cleared just enough space to stand beside the coffin. With Troy already there, it was a tight squeeze as I edged in next to him. Together, we stared down at the warped wood.

"Do you want to open it, or do you want me to?" he asked.

I sucked in my bottom lip and chewed on it. I'd been around a lot of dead bodies, but not ones that were over a hundred years old, and I wasn't thrilled with the idea of seeing the skeleton.

"Scared?" he asked.

"No. I'll open it." I wasn't sure why Troy made me so competitive.

I fumbled with the latches. It was old and not built like the coffins I was used to. Once it was unlatched, Troy helped me lift the lid.

I took a deep breath and peeked in. It was empty.

"What?" I exclaimed. "They took the whole body? What is the point of that?"

Troy shook his head. "I don't know."

"How could an entire body disappear?" I muttered to myself.

I looked around the empty coffin, but all that was there was a bit of dirt. And something small and brown. I reached out to grab it, and Troy grabbed my arm.

"Wait. Put this on." He reached into his pocket and pulled out a glove.

I pulled off my digging gloves, took the sterile one, and pulled it on. Then I grabbed the brown thing and held it up.

Troy studied it. "What is it?"

"An acrylic nail."

"I'm guessing those weren't a thing in the eighteen-hundreds."

"I doubt it belonged to Harrison—and eww. I think the real fingernail is attached to it. It has dry blood on it."

Troy climbed out of the grave and held out his hand. I grabbed it and he pulled me out. "That will make it easier to identify." He went to his things and grabbed a baggie and held it open. I dropped the fingernail inside, and he zipped it shut.

Murphy had worn himself out and was napping under a tree. I wished I could join him. I sat down and rolled my head around, listening to my neck crack.

"We need help," Troy said. "That took hours."

"What if I hire some people and the mortuary pays them?"

Troy nodded. "That or we need some machinery." His eyes narrowed. "I know a guy with equipment. Let me call and ask him if he'd be willing to be on the payroll for a few days."

I sat next to Murphy and rubbed my hands together, trying to get them to stop shaking.

An hour later, I saw Steve roll toward us on a mini excavator. Steve did a little of everything around town. I drew up an application on my phone and had him fill it out, then ran to the morgue to add him to the payroll. Once there, I ate a sandwich and made one for Troy.

By the time I got back down, Steve had dug up most of the coffin Troy had started on. I handed Troy the sandwich, and we sat and waited.

"It's pretty lame Walt makes people dig by hand," Troy said. "Look how fast he's going."

"I'm going to have to talk to him. This is much more efficient."

Steve jumped off the excavator and came over. "You'll have to get the top dirt off by hand."

"Thanks," I told him. "Do you think you could do more, or come back tomorrow?"

"Sure. I've been telling Walt for years that I could save him time. I have time tomorrow."

He drove the excavator slowly over to the road.

"Let's check the coffin," Troy said, jumping into his hole. "It's not latched."

I heard the lid creak open, and Troy's eyes narrowed. "Mine has a body."

"You win."

He pulled on a pair of gloves and looked around. I didn't feel the need to see inside. If I got down there, I would only be in the way.

"Have you gotten ahold of Harrison's sister?" I asked.

"Tori Callister? Nope. I have an address, but no phone number. She lives about two hours away, so I'm hoping to get some time to drive there. I tried to have officers go to her place, but she's never home."

Troy's phone rang from his backpack.

"Can you get that?" he asked. "Tell whoever it is I'll call them back, unless it's an emergency."

I grabbed his bag and pulled the phone from the pocket. The screen said Harmony Landing. Chase's family owned the Harmony Landing Hotel. I hesitated. It was probably Chase, and what would he say if I answered Troy's phone?

I pushed the button and put it to my ear. "Sheriff Mc-Gregor's phone. He's in the middle of something. Can I tell him something?"

"Oh... uh... hi," said a woman's voice. "Will you tell him it's Harmony?"

I covered the speaker with my thumb. "It's someone named Harmony."

He groaned. "Is she okay?"

"He wants to know if you're okay."

She laughed. "I guess I do only call him when I'm in peril. I'm fine. Will you ask him if he likes blue or green better?"

"He likes green."

"Shouldn't you ask him?"

I rolled my eyes. "Sheriff, do you like blue or green better?"

"Green."

"He said green."

"Great. Thanks."

"Bye." I hung up. That had been confusing. He was focused on something in the coffin. I didn't want to distract him by asking why someone named Harmony wanted to know what color he liked. It was also confusing that someone named Harmony would call from the Harmony Landing Hotel.

"Did she say why she wanted to know my favorite color?" he asked.

"No."

"It said Harmony Landing. She works at the hotel?"

"She owns the hotel. She bought it from Aunt Cathy a while back." We all called Cathy our aunt. At least, I used to.

"That's funny. Her name is actually Harmony?"

"Yep. That's why she bought the hotel."

"Weird. Does she usually call with vague questions?"

"No. She's great at finding trouble. She keeps Chase on his toes, too." He laughed.

"Chase?"

"Yeah, I told you he got married? Harmony is his wife."

"Oh," I said, trying not to sound relieved. Not that Troy wasn't allowed to have women call him. It was none of my business. I didn't care, but maybe my shoulders relaxed half an inch.

"There are lots of indents in the material lining the coffin," he said. "I think there were jewels or something on here. If you hand me my phone, I'll take some pictures and we can compare the things we found in the attic to the imprints here. I'm going to block this entire area off so we don't have to rebury things yet. We can put up some protective coverings. I worry we might have to dig it up again and we don't want to waste time."

I walked around, looking at the other graves. A stone next to the last-disturbed one had several pots full of red and orange pansies in front of it. I looked at the inscription. It was another Brightman grave. It was too old to have someone leaving flowers.

I kneeled and picked up a pot full of pansies. Underneath, the grass and dirt were disturbed.

"Hey, Sheriff? I think someone started digging here and didn't get far."

He came over and looked at the spot. "That might be a good thing. We can dig it up and see if there is anything odd inside."

"We should do it now."

"I'm going to have to talk to the judge again. I only said six graves."

"We don't have time for that. Let's dig this one, and not one of the others."

"I'll call the judge and see if we can make a substitution."

I hated waiting to do things the legal way. Especially when someone was clearly one step ahead of us.

Chapter 10

"Is this legal, hon?" Jessa asked.

I shrugged as I adjusted the big battery-powered light. "Probably not."

Roberta leaned on a shovel. "I feel like Jessica Fletcher. We're going to solve a mystery!"

"If we don't dig up this grave, someone else might. We need to see if anything's in there."

Jessa grabbed a shovel and looked up at the moon. "I can think of a lot better use of the night."

"You don't have to stay," I said, picking up a shovel. My arms still felt like spaghetti from all the earlier shoveling.

She smiled. "I know, but I don't want to be left out."

"Ouch!" Roberta muttered. "I got my foot."

Jessa laughed. "Already?"

"I'm never going to be graceful, that's for sure. My parents put me in ballet when I was young. I fell and knocked another girl's tooth out. That was the end of that."

I smiled and began digging. I cringed as my entire body protested.

"We might not be able to do this," I admitted. "The dirt here is a lot harder than on the other grave I dug. This one hasn't been disturbed, so it's packed hard."

"Don't give up yet," Jessa said. "I'm tougher than I look." She jabbed her shovel into the ground and jumped on it, digging more in one go than I had in three.

"Do we have to be quiet?" Roberta asked. "No one's anywhere near, right?"

"They shouldn't be," I said. Most of the town was a mile down the road. We could probably yell at the top of our lungs and no one would notice.

"I think manual labor's easier with a song."

"Oh! Me too," Jessa said. "*This Little Light of Mine*?"

Roberta nodded, and the two of them burst into song.

I dug and wished I had earplugs. Jessa had an incredible voice, but Roberta... not so much. Roberta sang loudly and about as-off key as you could get. It never bothered Jessa, though. She just kept singing like it was the most beautiful thing anyone's ever heard. They often sang in the flower shop when things were slow.

I was already tired with a slight headache, and I wasn't sure how long I would last. I didn't have to worry about the singing, because it didn't take long until we were all huffing as we dug. I couldn't gauge time, but by the time we'd uncovered the grave, it had been a good part of the night. Without Jessa, it never would have happened.

"Are we going to look inside?" Roberta asked.

"That's the plan," I said, unlatching the coffin. My head was throbbing now, and so was most of my body.

Roberta jumped out, and Jessa and I pushed the lid up.

"Gross, gross," Roberta said, closing her eyes.

I tried to avoid the skeleton and looked at all the jewelry surrounding the body. "Wow. That's a lot of jewelry."

"No kidding," Jessa said. "Now what?"

I scrunched my nose. "I'm not sure. We can't leave it where anyone could find it, but we shouldn't touch it. I'll stay here and guard it. In the morning, I'll call the sheriff."

"You can't stay here alone," Jessa said. "And what will you do if someone comes?"

"Call Troy. I'll be fine. You two go home and get some sleep. The shop is still going to be closed tomorrow, but Troy said we can clean it now that forensics has been over it. We can do that after lunch."

Roberta yawned. "I won't say no to going to bed. I might have to shower first. I smell like a gym sock."

I watched them leave, and I sat myself up against a tree. This was going to be a boring few hours until morning. I should have brought Murphy, but he'd been sound asleep when I left. I was beginning to think he spent most of his life asleep.

It had been a long time since I'd been out at night in the quiet. The bright stars twinkled at me as I tried to make out constellations. My eyes felt a little blurry, so I closed them. It would only be for a minute.

The next thing I knew, someone was picking me up. I almost panicked… until I recognized Troy.

The sun was rising, and there were officers surrounding the coffin we'd dug up.

"Put me down," I muttered.

He ignored me and began walking toward the morgue.

"Jessa had a bout of guilt and called me," he said. "She was worried a thief might come take you and the coffin."

I held my head stiffly up and grimaced at the pain in my neck. I put one arm around his neck so I wouldn't fall.

"I can walk."

"I doubt it. You should see your eyes. They can't even focus."

"Believe me, I know," I mumbled. "You can't carry me up the hill."

"Sure I can."

I gave up and tried to rest my head on his shoulder. My arm was in the way, so my face ended up awkwardly in his neck. I wasn't one hundred percent sure this was happening and not a dream. Everything felt a bit off, but

I supposed that's what happened when you only slept a couple of hours at night.

He smelled good. I probably smelled like sweat, or a gym sock, like Roberta said.

"I stink," I muttered.

He chuckled. "You've smelled worse."

"I'd kick you, but it sounds exhausting."

This was why we never would've worked out, even if he had liked me that way. Our relationship was still as immature as it had been fifteen years ago.

Troy went quiet as he walked up the hill. He was probably tired. He'd done a lot of digging yesterday, too. I was going to protest again when he carried me up the steps and to my room, but I was almost sure I was half asleep.

Murphy barked, but it was in the back of my mind.

Troy leaned over and placed me on my bed. His cheek brushed against my lips—at least I think it was his cheek—and I rolled over and hoped he hadn't noticed. If he did, he didn't say anything. He pulled the blanket over me, and I kept my eyes tight shut.

"Do you need anything?" he asked.

"Feed Murphy," I mumbled.

I heard him open the bag of dog food and pour it into the bowl. He closed the curtains and left the room. I was sure he was saving a lecture for when I was conscious enough to hear it.

I had one weird dream after another and finally forced myself to get up when Murphy jumped on the bed a few hours later.

"Oh, man. I hurt everywhere. I was not meant to be a gravedigger."

Murphy sat on my lap and wagged his little tail.

I climbed out of bed and rubbed Murphy's head. "Look what I did to my sheets. They're covered in dirt." Murphy's tongue hung out, and he almost looked as if he were smiling. "I'm going to take a shower, then I'll take you outside." I'd put a litter box in my room, but so far Murphy seemed good at holding it.

Each step sent pain shooting from my foot to my hip, and reaching out to turn on the shower hurt my shoulder. By the time I was ready for the day, it was already afternoon.

I grabbed Murphy, and we went to the flower shop. Jessa and Roberta were already there. Murphy ran through the fallen flower petals and pushed them around with his nose.

"Sorry I'm late," I said.

"We figured you would be, so we came late," Roberta said. Her blouse buttons were unevenly buttoned, but she didn't care about things like that. I'd told her once, and she told me it gave her more character. "I've never been this sore in my life."

I grabbed a broom and started sweeping. There was nothing to do but ignore the pain that ran down my arms and back.

"I called the sheriff," Jessa said. "I was worried about you. Was he mad?"

I kept sweeping. "Who knows? I was too delirious to have a normal conversation. I don't think he said anything about it."

"I think the sheriff misses your friendship," Roberta said, wiping flower petals from the counter into the garbage.

I laughed. "Why would you think that?"

"Sometimes he looks at you and his eyes are sad."

"I've noticed that," Jessa agreed.

"You two don't know what you're talking about. He just doesn't know what to do about me."

"Do we have any orders today?" Roberta asked.

"No. We've been closed so much this week and no one has been answering the phone. All the orders we have are advanced ones and I don't think any of them come due until next week."

"Someone just pulled up," Jessa said, looking out the window. "I don't recognize the car."

"Great." I swept faster and pushed as much of the mess as I could behind the counter. I didn't want a new customer to see this.

A woman with short brown hair and wiry limbs came strolling in. Her skirt was a little short, and her blouse could do with a few more buttons being fastened. Her five-inch heels made her appear awkward as she stumbled and waved her arms around. My guess: the shoes were new.

"Hello," she said, smiling. "I'm lost. Am I anywhere near the mortuary?"

"It's up the hill," I told her, pointing. "It's closed right now. I can help if you need something. My grandpa owns it."

"Oh, then you must know my brothers. Harrison and Mitchel?"

I shared a look with Jessa. "Yes."

"Do you know where I can get ahold of them? They seem to be ignoring my calls."

"Umm... I think the sheriff has been trying to get ahold of you."

She narrowed her eyes. "Of me? Why?"

I wasn't sure if I should say, or have Troy do it. "Why don't you let me call him and have him meet you here?"

"I can't imagine why a sheriff in a town I've never been to would want to talk to me."

"It's about your brother."

She raised her brow. "Oh?"

"I'm sorry to be the one to tell you this, but Harrison is dead."

She tilted her head. "What do you mean 'dead?'"

I guessed she didn't actually want a definition of dead, so I shrugged. "I'm sorry."

She put her hands over her face, and my eyes focused on her long, brown fingernails. Two were missing, and both fingers were wrapped in band-aids.

"You stay here. I'll get the sheriff." I scooped up Murphy and hurried from the shop. I went around the hill to the cemetery, moving slower than usual. It was crawling with police. I wondered if they brought some in from another county.

I scanned the area looking for Troy and finally spotted him giving some officers orders. He saw me and came over.

"Harrison's sister is at the flower shop."

He took a deep breath. "Nice. It's about time something fell into place."

"She has long, fake brown fingernails."

"Oh?"

"Two are missing, and she has band-aids."

His eyes lit up. "That means she was digging here."

"She said she's never been to town before, but Mitchel told me she'd been here."

"You didn't interrogate her, did you?"

"No. I'm only forcing myself to be alive today. It's all I can take."

"Let's go. Peterson? You're in charge. I'll be back soon."

A man nodded, and we walked back together.

"For such a small dog, you sure are heavy," I told Murphy.

"Why are you carrying him?"

"He's slow, and he wanders. I don't know a lot about pugs, but this one does his own thing." I paused a moment. "Is there a reason you're still holding my grandpa? There are so many other people who look more guilty."

He rubbed his hand over the back of his head and sighed. "They look more guilty of grave robbing, but he still looks more guilty of murder. I honestly don't think he did it now, but with the time I have, I can't focus there yet. I would if he were unhappy, but he's having a great time."

"It seems that way."

"He should retire. He would probably enjoy it."

"He's past the age, but he won't. It's driving Jerry crazy."

"Something's off with Jerry. He shouldn't be avoiding me. There are so many things happening and not enough resources. I need deputies here every day, but there are other places I need them as well."

"I thought you might arrest me."

He grinned. "I should. I called the judge and explained the mix-up in the graves, and he was okay with it."

"Mix-up?"

He shrugged.

We entered the shop, and Troy asked us if we would let him talk to Tori in private. Jessa, Roberta, and I went outside. Murphy ran after a butterfly.

"What's going on?" Jessa asked.

"The sheriff and I found a long brown fingernail that matches Harrison's sister's in a grave."

"You mean you left us alone with a murderer?"

"She's probably not a murderer. Just a grave robber."

Roberta shivered. "That's such a strange thing to do."

Jessa nodded and rubbed her arm. "And a lot of effort."

"Let's take a break," I said, sinking into a chair.

"But we've hardly done anything," Roberta said, sitting next to me.

"You two are too soft," Jessa said. "It was just a little digging. Walk it off."

The door slammed open as Tori rushed out. She stomped to her car, got in, and slammed the door. Her tires squealed as she drove away.

Troy came out and rubbed his eyes.

"I take it things went well?" I said with a small smile.

"She's going to be fun to work with. I told her she needs to stay in town, but with that exit, I'm worried."

"I'll tell ya one thing," Jessa said, "she did not seem like a woman who had just discovered her brother died. She gave a few fake tears, then started talking about her weekend in Sacramento."

Roberta nodded. "She didn't seem shocked by the mess in the store, either."

Troy glanced at me. "We've gotten everything we can from the mortuary. It can open. I'll take down all the crime scene tape."

"I'm not opening without Grandpa, or at least Jerry. I can't do both of their jobs. Though it will be nice not to have to avoid certain areas. Are you still going to stay there?"

"If that's okay? It saves a lot of time not having to drive back and forth."

"That's fine." I'd hardly noticed he was there. He must've been eating in town. I probably should have offered to feed him while he was there, but that would feel weird. Eating with him would be too much.

Chapter 11

The microwave beeped, and I pulled out my breakfast burrito. I was beginning to wonder if I wanted to spend my life living in the morgue. I told myself it was fine, but was it? If I did, there would need to be some serious remodeling.

The dark kitchen was decorated in gray and black. I sometimes wondered if Grandpa wanted the place to look eerie and unwelcoming, because that's what it was.

My room was the only room in the house with colorful curtains and bedding. I had amazing pictures on the walls to cheer up the dreary paint, and I paid to have thick, light brown carpet installed. I should paint the walls, but I knew the dark paint would be hard to cover.

My uncle entered, appearing nonchalant.

"Uncle Jerry! Where have you been?" I grabbed a fork and sat at the small round table.

He shrugged. "There was no reason to hang around here when the cops were running things."

"I know Sheriff McGregor has been trying to get a hold of you."

He opened the pantry and stared inside. "I don't have time to talk to him."

"I'm not sure it's a choice. He needs to talk to everyone who was around here when the murder happened. If you avoid him, it might make you look guilty."

He sighed and pulled out a half-eaten bag of chips. "I guess I could talk to him for a few minutes. You know I was in the city when it happened."

"He's staying here during the investigation. In Aunt Gina's old room."

"That's just great," he grumbled. "I hate having house-guests."

"You know him. It's not like he's a stranger. He spent a lot of time here when I was growing up," I reminded him.

Uncle Jerry's eyes narrowed. "Whatever happened to you and your friends? You three were thicker than thieves, and then one day, they never came around again."

"We grew apart," I said, cutting my burrito.

"Hmm. You seemed pretty upset."

I was surprised Jerry had noticed anything. He'd never paid a lot of attention to me. "It was a long time ago."

"Grandpa hates him."

"Yeah, but he hates most people."

"He thinks there's some big dark secret that you won't talk about. I figured you just realized the crush you had on one of them hadn't gone anywhere and you were heartbroken."

I stared at my uncle. Maybe he was more observant than I'd ever thought.

"That's ridiculous," I said, taking a bite.

"Is it?"

There was a knock on the door, and Troy poked his head in. "Jerry, I saw your truck. Can we talk for a minute in private?"

"I don't talk in private. You can come in and say what you want."

Troy nodded, and I motioned to the chair next to me. He sat, and Jerry took the chair across from him.

I stood and got them both a soda. I should've left, but I wanted to know what Jerry would say.

I settled back down and kept an eye on them.

Jerry leaned against his chair and popped a chip into his mouth.

"I'm sorry I have to ask these things, but I have to talk to everyone who was in the house when Harrison was killed."

"I wasn't in the house."

"But you have no proof, so I still need to ask."

"Then ask."

"Where were you when Harrison was killed?"

"How am I supposed to know? I don't memorize where I am from day to day. I was in the city, that's all I know. I didn't kill him, and that's what you need to know, right?"

Troy had always been a little wary around my uncle, but if he still was, he hid it well.

"If you could try to remember, that would be great. Then I could get others to confirm it."

"I was probably at the movie theater or the diner."

"Do you have any receipts? Parking stubs?"

"I threw them away."

"Did you see anyone acting suspicious that day? Before you went to the city?"

"Nope." He popped another chip into his mouth.

"Do you have any suspicions?"

"No."

"Have you seen anything suspicious in the cemetery?" Troy pushed.

"Nobody was killed in the cemetery."

I wanted to make a joke, but I knew it wasn't the time.

"Some things have happened in the cemetery, and I'm looking into them as well."

His eye twitched. "I don't know anything."

"Come on, Uncle Jerry," I said. "Could you at least try to answer the questions?"

He crossed his arms. "Why does he get to ask all the questions?"

Troy's expression didn't change. "You can ask me questions."

"Why are you into everyone's business?"

I rolled my eyes. "He's the sheriff. It's his job."

"Fine. What did you do to make my niece hate you so completely?"

Troy flinched, and my stomach dropped.

"I don't hate him," I protested.

"Sure you do. You leave the room anytime someone mentions the sheriff."

Troy clenched his jaw, and I wanted to punch my uncle.

I took a deep breath. "That doesn't mean I hate him."

"Then what happened? Everyone in town has wondered for years."

"That isn't what he's here to talk about. He didn't do anything, I just overreacted to something, and I've regretted it ever since." There. I'd admitted it.

Troy's frown receded, and he turned back to my uncle. "I need to know where you were. If you want to think and talk later, that's fine."

Jerry shrugged and got up. "If anything comes to me, I'll let you know." He grabbed the chip bag and left.

"Sorry about that," I said.

He opened his soda. "That's about how I figured it would go." He took a drink and looked at me. "You overreacted?" he asked softly, his eyes probing mine.

I looked at the table. The last time I'd told him what happened, I'd been screaming, and I wasn't really sure what I'd said. I wasn't a crier, but there was a definite lump in my throat.

"Chase was going out of town. You said we should get dinner. I thought, great, that will be fun." I didn't tell him I stressed myself out, wondering if he'd meant it as a date or just like everything else we did together.

"Then you talked to Quincy?"

I looked up. "Yeah. I ran into her, and she asked what I was doing that night. I told her we were going to dinner. She said, 'Oh, right. Troy told me. He said once he went on a date with you, he could say he'd dated everyone in our graduating class.' I was so mad."

"I never even talked to Quincy. I didn't tell anyone we were going to dinner."

I swallowed. "I'm sorry. I saw red. We spent years making fun of all the girls who tried to throw themselves at you and Chase. When I heard what Quincy said, I thought you were lumping me in with all of those girls. I thought our friendship was more solid than that. Nothing reasonable went through my head. I was just so angry."

"I'm sorry you felt that way," he said. "I promise I never said that."

I nodded. "I knew I overreacted, but I was embarrassed for yelling at you, so instead of apologizing, I just let myself get angrier. It was easier to blame it on you."

He stood and tossed his can in the trash. "Can we start over?"

I got to my feet and nodded. "I should probably apologize to Chase as well. I'm just not sure I'm up for it this week."

He held out his hand. "So, we're friends again?"

I took his hand. "Friends." Why was that such a painful word?

Troy pulled me in and gave me a hug. I wrapped my arms around him and sighed. It was familiar, but different. He definitely lifted more than five-pound weights. That wasn't what I needed to be focused on. It had been a long time since anyone had hugged me. My family wasn't into hugging.

I pulled away and gave him a half grin. "I guess I don't have to avoid Crystal Rock anymore."

He groaned. "I'm sorry it was that bad for you. I thought it was hard on Chase and me, but you didn't have anyone."

"But it was my fault."

I wanted to tell him how lonely I'd been, but I didn't want him to know how pathetic my life could be.

Troy smiled. "We won't worry about it anymore, alright? Let's go find us a graverobber."

"Right now?"

He shrugged. "Why not?"

"Any ideas?"

"Tori's staying with Mitchel. Do you want to go talk to her with me?"

"Is that allowed?"

He shrugged.

"What's happening at the cemetery?"

"My people have cleaned it all up. Lots of results should be coming back anytime now. I'm hoping to get some fingerprint matches from the gun and maybe the attic and flower shop. It's taking longer than I thought."

We drove to the trailer park and went to Mitchel's door. He opened it and let out a slow breath. "Both of you at the same time? This is ridiculous."

"I need to talk to Tori," Troy said.

"Oh, good. Come in, I'll get her."

We sat on the couch and waited. Tori came out and glared at us.

"Sit," Mitchel told her.

"I'm not talking to anyone." She sank down on a chair, and Mitchel stood against the wall with his arms crossed.

"You're welcome to get a lawyer," Troy told her.

"I don't need a lawyer, because I didn't do anything."

"You dug up graves. That's illegal."

"Why would I do that?"

Troy clasped his hands together and rested his elbows on his knees. "Your missing fingernail was in one of the coffins. It looked just like yours and you're missing some."

She fiddled with her band-aid. "That could've been any-one's nail. Lots of people have them. Mocha mousse is one of the most common colors at the moment."

"But the actual fingernail, which ripped off with the fake one, will easily identify it as yours."

She took a shaky breath and looked at Mitchel.

He shrugged. "Don't look at me. Get out of your own mess."

She cursed under her breath and muttered something about unsupportive siblings. "I broke my nails while I was getting things out of my trunk. And it only broke the fake ones off, not my real ones."

Troy's gaze never left her face. "Was anyone with you when it happened?"

"Only Harrison."

Mitchel snorted. "Well, that's convenient."

Her eyes went wide. "Harrison must have taken it and tried to frame me! I bet he dug up the graves and tossed the nail in there."

"Oh sure. Blame the dead guy. That's classy."

"I'm serious! I was getting groceries out of my trunk, and the nails caught on something. I would have no reason to dig up graves! I've never even been to this town before."

Mitchel shook his head. "That's a lie. Harrison told me you were staying with him last week."

"He was the liar. He must have planned everything with the intention of blaming me. I bet he was behind every-thing."

Troy frowned. "He sure didn't shoot himself."

"Are you blaming me for that?" she asked, clenching her fists.

"No, I'm only saying he didn't do everything."

I stood. "Will you all excuse me? I need to go take a call."

No one was paying attention to me. I went outside and looked around the trailer park. There was no way to guess which one had been Harrison's. I walked around until I saw one with a padlock on the door.

"Bingo," I muttered. I went around to the back and looked in the garbage can. Troy had probably gone through it all. I tried to remember if this was a garbage-pickup week. We only get it picked up every other week because we're such a small town. I don't pay a lot of attention to things like that. There was enough garbage to convince me it wasn't until this Friday.

I moved a few things around, but I wasn't in the mood to get the smelly garbage all over me. If I'd thought no one had been through it, I would, but there was no way the police wouldn't have searched it.

Checking to see if the backdoor was locked was proba-bly a waste of time, but I did it anyway.

Locked.

I stood on the wooden porch and sighed, pausing. A dirty footprint marked the porch rail. Why would anyone stand there... unless they were hiding something up high? I wondered why I was wearing my high-heeled boots. That complicated things.

I placed my foot on the support bar in the middle of the rail and climbed to the top, using the porch light to support myself. I knew the chances of it breaking off were high if I put too much weight on it, so I stepped carefully. The board my foot was on was four inches wide; it was hardly a challenge—at least that was what I told myself.

With an upward reach, I explored the rain gutter with my hand. Old wet leaves touched my fingers, and I tried not to think about the gross creepy crawlies that might be in there. I moved my hand a little further and my fingertips touched something soft and slightly textured. It was wedged, like someone had shoved it there in a panic.

I went on my toes. Every time I tried to pull it out with the two fingers that could actually reach it, it would get stuck on the side and I would lose it.

On what felt like the tenth try, it came up and fell to the ground.

Hands grabbed me around the waist.

I screamed as they lifted me down to my feet. Running on instinct, I spun and punched.

Troy dodged my hit. "Whoa!"

I took a deep breath and put my hand on my heart. "Troy! What are you doing? You almost gave me a heart attack!"

"You should have seen yourself up there. You looked like you were about to go over the side. I didn't dare say anything because I thought it would scare you and make you fall."

He still had his hands on my waist, so I moved away and went down the three steps to the ground.

"I found this in the rain gutter," I said, picking up a worn leather wallet. I handed it to Troy, and he opened it and pulled out a sandwich baggie full of cash.

"What made you climb up there?"

"There was a footprint on the rail." I pointed.

Troy shook his head. "I think the reason I'm no good at my job is because I'm not crazy."

"What are you talking about? You're great at your job."

He shook his head. "I'm not sure. I keep missing things in my cases lately because I don't think to do things like climb a rail and stick my hand in a rain gutter."

"I'm sorry that I told you I was surprised you were sheriff when you first came. I'm really not. You're a good guy, Troy. All the people love you, because you care about them."

"That doesn't mean I make the best decisions."

"Climbing on the rail probably wasn't the best decision."

"No, but it got results." He huffed out a breath. "It's fine. I'm done pitying myself. Come on, let's drive back and I'll get you a donut."

Chapter 12

"Get off my face," I mumbled, pushing Murphy onto my pillow. He turned and drooled on my cheek. "Nasty." I wiped it on the pillowcase since I was going to have to change it anyway.

Murphy barked, and I sat up.

"We need some rules here, bud. This is *my* bed." I pointed to the cozy dog bed in the corner. "That is Murphy's bed. If we're going to have good sleep, you need to respect that."

Murphy climbed onto my lap and stared up at me. I smiled and rubbed his jowls. Who could resist such an adorable, scrunchy face?

I got ready and ate breakfast. There was no sign of Jerry or Troy. Jerry was probably in the basement working, and

Troy had enough on his plate to keep him constantly engaged.

I needed to finish cleaning the flower shop. Since we'd been interrupted, we hadn't finished.

A thump above me caused me to freeze. Not again.

I put my bowl in the sink and looked around for a better weapon than a folded-up camp chair. The kitchen had plenty of knives, but I felt more comfortable with something bigger and easier to swing. I went quietly to my room and grabbed the bat.

It would be stupid to not call Troy, so I dialed him and went to voicemail. "I think there's someone in the attic," I whispered. Whoever was up there probably thought the place was empty. "I'm going up." I stuck the phone in my pocket and went to my aunt's old room.

The squeak the closet made when I opened it made me cringe. I didn't want to announce I was coming. I slipped up the ladder, being careful of the bat. The trapdoor was opened, which meant whoever was up there had come through this way.

I peeked out the top. It was clear. At least this tower.

I tiptoed down the staircase and peered around the corner into the attic. I couldn't see anyone. No noises, nothing. If someone had been up here, they must have left while I was grabbing the bat. Coming out early could be bad, so I waited. It felt like forever, but was probably only a minute. I counted to one hundred for good measure.

I stepped into the attic.

The sun shone in the window, making me squint.

Someone plowed into me from the side, knocking me to the floor, and causing me to drop the bat. I rolled over and shoved a figure dressed in black. The person hit the floor, and I rolled the other way and scrambled upright.

The figure stood and swayed, but caught their balance.

"What are you doing?" I demanded. The person was shorter than me and had short brown hair poking out of their ski mask. From her shape, I could tell it was a woman.

She took a step back, and I charged forward, knocking her back to the floor with my shoulder. She rolled away, grabbed my bat, and swung, smacking me in the shin.

I yelped as I hit the floor for the second time.

The woman scrambled to her feet and ran to the spiral stairs.

Pain exploded in my leg. I clutched it and gasped. No way I was catching her now. I thought about dropping through the trapdoor into the hallway. I probably would've if my leg wasn't already hurt. I crawled over to it and pulled the door back. I might be able to watch the person run by and get a better feel for who it was. Tori made sense... but something didn't sit right. What if I was wrong? I grabbed a rock from my collection and waited. Maybe it was good I hadn't cleaned it up.

Footsteps tearing down the hall made me hold my breath. The woman ran under me and I chucked the rock, nailing her in the neck. She let out a small shriek and ran out of sight.

I stood and cringed at the pain in my leg. Nothing was broken, but I was going to have an impressive bruise.

My eyes swept the attic.

I grinned when I saw a phone on the ground. She must have lost it in the struggle. I picked it up and pushed the button. A familiar pug stared up at me from the lock screen—Murphy. My Murphy. I tried a few obvious passwords, and the phone locked me out.

I stuck it in my back pocket and climbed back down into Aunt Gina's room. I would always think of it as her room. She'd lived here most of my younger years. She still stayed here when she visited at Christmas. I wasn't sentimental. We'd never been close. Still, it felt like her room. That's probably why I'd avoided it and never found the easy way up to the attic.

Every step made my leg throb, but I told myself I just needed to walk it off. When I got to the hallway, I heard steps tearing to the top of the stairs. Troy ran into the hallway and skidded to a stop when he saw me. He bent down, rested his hands on his thighs, and took deep breaths.

"Are you okay?" he asked through panting breaths. "I got your message and ran from the cemetery."

"Why were you there?" I ignored his question.

"The judge said we could dig up all the graves with the Brightman last name. Did you go to the attic? You shouldn't do things like that."

"Someone attacked me up there. It was definitely a woman. She got away."

"You hear a noise? You *run* and you call me. That's it," he scolded.

"I called. You didn't answer."

He stood tall. "Then you should have left and gotten help."

"I got this." I pulled the phone from my pocket and handed it to him. "She dropped it."

His eyes lit up. "Nice. This could solve everything."

"I tried to guess the password, so it's locked for the next minute or so. It has a picture of Murphy on it."

"Interesting. Who would have that on their phone?"

I smiled. "I bet it was Tori. Whoever it was had a mask, but I saw some short brown hair sticking out at the side. Since she's Harrison's sister, she might have a picture of his dog."

"Sounds right. We were already leaning toward her being behind some things. I can't imagine why she would come in here and shoot Harrison, though. And how did she figure out how to get to the attic? Especially since we didn't know about those ways and we'd been up there a ton."

I shrugged. "I have no clue."

"I've gotten some things back."

"Oh?"

"The only fingerprints on the gun were your grandpa's and Jerry's."

My eyebrows came together.

"Don't worry," he said. "It could have been someone wearing gloves. The attic only had the prints of people who make sense because they live here, and some of mine. The flower shop was the same. Only people who work there, except in the areas customers touch, and then there were tons. None of the coffins had prints, except where we touched them, so whoever robbed them had gloves."

"So, nothing helpful?"

"Not really. I was discouraged, but the phone could make all the difference." He looked at the screen. "Nice. We can try more passwords."

"Maybe it's not a number, but a word."

"In reality, I have to get a warrant to try to search it."

I snatched it from his hand. "I don't." I looked at the screen and tried to think.

"I'm going to make a call," Troy said. "I need someone searching the town for the person who came in."

He moved over to the side, and I stared at the picture of Murphy. It couldn't be that easy... I typed in "Murphy," and the phone unlocked.

"Score," I mumbled as I looked for any sign of who the phone belonged to. I went to the text messages and tapped one that was listed as 'hottie.'

I felt a little guilty reading someone's texts, but not enough to not read them, especially as my shin throbbed in reminder of her attack. I began reading the most recent conversation.

Hottie: *Stop ignoring me.*

Hottie: *Harrison? Answer me.*

I paused. Did that mean the phone was Harrison's? It must.

Harrison: *I'm busy.*

Hottie: *Call me.*

Harrison: *Can't.*

Hottie: *I've done a lot for you. You better pay me.*

Harrison: *Calm down. I told you, I will.*

Hottie: *I know you have the money.*

Harrison: *I hid it. I can't get to it right now.*

Hottie: *I knew I shouldn't trust you.*

Harrison: *Don't get dramatic.*

Hottie: *I swear I wanna kill you right now.*

Harrison: *Don't be like that.*

The message ended, and I went to the next message. It was labeled as 'the man.' This was ridiculous. Why couldn't he put a name in?

The man: *You got my money?*

Harrison: *Tomorrow.*

The man: *What's wrong with today?*

Harrison: *Too many people around. You want your dad-dy to find out?*

The man: *Getting tired of you.*

Harrison: *LOL. Who isn't?*

The man: *You won't be laughing for long.*

The next messages were from Mitchel.

Mitchel: *Why do I ever listen to you? I hate this job.*

Harrison: *Give it one more month.*

Mitchel: *I hate you.*

Harrison sure wasn't getting any love. I scrolled to Tori's name.

Tori: *You always drag me down.*

Harrison: *Stop whining. You're such a baby.*

Tori: *I've done some seriously dangerous stuff for you. Are you going to pay me?*

Harrison: *Don't I always?*

Tori: *It's not worth it anymore.*

Harrison: *Fine. I'll keep your cut.*

Tori: *Fine. Watch your back, bro.*

"What are you reading?" Troy asked, scaring me from my reading.

"Texts. This is Harrison's phone. Everyone texting him seems to hate him. I think there might be several people who were working with him. I'm not sure if they're talking about the grave robbing, but it looks like it." I added, "So, whoever was in the attic stole his phone."

"That's my guess."

My shoulders sagged in relief. "Then they probably killed him, which means it wasn't Grandpa."

He nodded. "Probably. Look, Neeley. I told Walt he could go yesterday. He told me he knows his rights, and he's not going anywhere."

My eyes narrowed. "That doesn't make sense."

"Not at all. I'm telling you. Walt needs to retire. He's sitting in the cell reading, eating, and watching TV all day long. He's worked himself so hard he thinks he deserves a vacation. In jail."

I pushed my bangs to the side. "I'll talk to him."

"I really want to read those texts."

I held out the phone.

"I can't. I could get in a lot of trouble without a warrant."

"Fine. Walk me to the flower shop, I'll read them to you on the way."

"I'm not sure that makes it okay."

"I didn't say I was giving you a choice."

He grinned, and we left the morgue. I read the texts as we went, and Troy tried to appear uninterested, but I could tell he was taking it all in. When we got to the shop, I handed him the phone.

"Alright, now go get your warrant."

"I will. Thanks. You're walking a little funny."

"Yeah, well, I got hit in the shin with a baseball bat."

"What? Let me see."

"Nah. It's fine. I'm going to ignore it and look at it later. I'm sure it will have an impressive bruise. If it does, I'll show it to you tomorrow."

I think Troy makes me immature. We used to compare bruises when we were young. No one had ever topped the bruise Chase got when he dropped a weight on his foot.

"I'm not sure I should leave you here alone," he said as we went inside.

"Jessa will be here in thirty minutes. I can't stay closed for long. I've been ignoring too many things I should be doing. I probably have a bunch of online orders I should be mailing out."

"Lock the door until Jessa comes."

"I should have opened ten minutes ago. I can't lock out customers."

"You can let people in if you recognize them."

"I might recognize the murderer."

"Don't let any suspects in."

"That's half the town, Troy."

He tilted his head. "Neeley…"

"I won't."

"Liar."

He still knew me like he used to, which was comforting… and a little dangerous.

Chapter 13

"Look at my wreath," Roberta said, proudly holding up a Valentine's Day masterpiece exploding with foamy pink and red hearts and... blue and purple daisies?

Roberta was a whiz with wreaths... as long as you gave her step-by-step instructions. When she freestyled? Well, let's just say her artistic vision wasn't for the faint of heart.

"Wow," Jessa said. "That's an... interesting color combo."

By interesting, I was sure she meant hideous or just plain ugly.

Confession time: when Roberta made wreaths like this, I'd wait until everyone left, gently dismantle them, and let her assume they'd sold. I didn't lie, exactly. She just didn't ever ask, and I didn't volunteer the truth. She was so proud of her creations, and I didn't have the heart to crush her. Besides, she never checked the website. It was easier to let the wreaths quietly disappear than break her spirit.

We were sitting in the back room making things for the online store. I wasn't sure, but it was beginning to look like we might start selling more online than in the shop. It was definitely easier to work with fake flowers.

"Is book club on tonight?" Jessa asked as she weaved flowers into her wreath.

"Yes. Do you think we have an addiction? I don't think most people have book club twice a week."

Jessa laughed. "We have a boring town, that's what we have. We have to make our own fun."

Roberta put her wreath on the table. "I haven't finished the first half of the book. I'm going to have to skim it before I come."

"Is the sheriff coming?" Jessa asked.

I paused, pretending to concentrate on the wreath in front of me, but the truth was, I wasn't sure. And I hated that I didn't know.

"Probably not," I said, trying to sound casual. "He's swamped. It's not exactly been a quiet week in Clover Haven."

"I guess that's right. I wonder how close they are to solving things." Jessa fiddled with a flower, twirling it between two fingers.

My mind was still stuck on Troy. I hated how a single question could leave me unsteady. I wished I didn't care if he showed up. I wished I didn't keep hoping he would.

I shrugged. "I feel almost confident I know who killed Harrison."

"Oh?"

"It had to be Tori. She had the missing nail, and today when someone attacked me, I was positive it was a woman, and she had short brown hair."

"Whoa, whoa, whoa," Jessa said. "Someone attacked you today?"

I caught them up on what had happened.

"I can see why you would think it was her. So why is she running around free, and Walt's still locked up?"

I groaned. "Grandpa likes being locked up. I should go talk to him, but I'm sure it won't get me anywhere."

The bell on the front door tinkled.

"I've got it," I said, putting down the vines I'd been cutting. I went to the front of the shop and saw Jerry. I frowned. He never came here.

"Hey, Neeley. I need to drive into Crystal Rock. Can you handle the phone?" He held out the mortuary cell phone, and I took it. We didn't get a lot of calls, but we made sure someone always had the phone with them.

"I can do that. What are you doing there?"

"I need a break. I'm going to the diner, then I might relax on the beach."

I nodded and watched him leave. I wondered what he needed a break from. He had done no work that I knew of since Harrison's murder.

"Hey, gals?" I called. "I'm going to run home for a minute."

"Okay," Jessa called back.

I rushed to the mortuary and straight up the stairs and into Jerry's room. I didn't know what he was up to, but something weird was going on with him. I figured now was the best time to go through his things.

I felt a bit guilty as I looked under his bed and in his closet. It turned out he had two closets. The one that goes up to the attic, and one for clothes. Jerry had scared me when I was a kid, so I'd stayed far away from his room.

Nothing seemed out of the ordinary, but I didn't look in his drawers, because that seems like crossing a line.

I pulled up his mattress and let out a breath. A sandwich baggie full of money had been stuffed there. It looked just like the bag and money in Harrison's rain gutter. I pulled out my phone and snapped a picture. I didn't dare take it.

I hated to think Jerry was involved.

By the time I put everything back exactly as I had found it and returned to the flower shop, only twenty minutes had passed.

"Look, Roberta made another wreath," Jessa said. "She's on a roll today."

I gave a tight smile as I looked at Roberta's creation. I was going to have to spend extra time taking them apart after work. It was fine. It made her happy to make them. I should probably put one on the door to the morgue. It would fit in with the odd feel of the place.

By the time Roberta and Jessa left, I'd convinced myself that Jerry might be guilty of killing Harrison over Tori. Jerry knew where Grandpa's gun was, and it was no secret he wanted him to retire so he could take over. If he killed Harrison, and Grandpa went to jail for it, everything would be his.

I wished I'd had more time with Harrison's phone. There might have been more texts that would give me some answers. Or I might've just ended up with more suspects. I wished I'd met Harrison at least once. Then I might have had a better feel for what he was like.

I went back to the morgue and let Murphy out of my room. We went to the kitchen and made a quick batch of brownies. I'd forgotten to assign dessert to the book club—again.

Upstairs, I slipped into my green drop-waist dress and straightened the cap sleeves, smoothing the fringe so it swayed just right. I only dressed up for book club once or twice a month, but this week's twenties theme deserved the full treatment.

I pinned back my bangs for the bell-shaped hat, then layered on strings of pearls and reached for the dark plum lipstick I only ever wore with this outfit. The black and purple bruise on my leg stood out, but it was nothing tights wouldn't hide. I hoped. I touched the tender spot and winced.

With my overdone smoky eye makeup done and my Mary Janes strapped on, I gave myself one last look in the mirror.

I brushed through my long dark hair, knowing I could never be a true flapper without bobbing my hair. That was never going to happen, but I still felt like I captured the look.

When the other members of the club began arriving, I was glad I'd dressed up. Some people dressed up every time, but everyone dressed up when it was a book set in the twenties. Jim even showed up in a pinstripe suit with a fedora and pocket watch.

"I smell brownies!" Jessa said, entering in her long, red silk dress. She wore a feathered headband and had a small purse at her side.

"Everyone in!" I commanded when the doorway got jammed. "We can talk inside."

They all entered and sat at the table. I left the lights on today, because with all the effort people put into their costumes, we shouldn't be hidden in dim candlelight.

Troy entered, and I covered my mouth to hold in a laugh. He was wearing almost the exact outfit Jim was wearing, but it fit a little small.

I went over and looked him up and down. "Nice outfit."

"Jim told me it was required. He made me borrow it." He paused. "I almost didn't recognize you. Your eyes are captivating." He coughed. "I mean, they always are. They're just... are those brownies?" He dashed to the table, and I wondered if I should take more time with my eye makeup in the mornings.

"I'm here!" Viola said, spinning into the room. She held her gloved hands in the air and made a dramatic bow. Viola was one of the few people who always dressed up. Her dress had more fringe and sequins than the rest of us put together.

Roberta came in after her. She made my six strings of pearls seem like nothing. She had at least twelve. There was no way that felt comfortable.

Lydia was the last to arrive. She had a serving tray full of small sandwiches, and was dressed as fancy as Viola. "I know I didn't have dessert today, but I made some cucumber sandwiches!"

"Wonderful!" I said, taking them and placing the tray on the table.

"I read the entire book," Billie informed us.

"Fine, but don't spoil anything past the first half," I told her.

Billie had been known to not follow that rule before, which had almost resulted in a fist-fight a few months ago.

"I know, I know."

Everyone began talking in small groups.

I sat next to Troy. "I'm surprised you made it," I whispered. "I thought you would be too busy."

"Everyone here was here during the murder. I need to keep an open mind and not rule anyone out."

I nodded. "I found a baggie of cash under Jerry's mattress. I was going to tell you, but I got distracted."

Troy's eyes narrowed. "Not good. Is he home?"

"No, but I bet he will be any time."

"I'm going to run and look. Will you be my lookout?"

"Sure." I stood and turned to the group. "You know how we all love cute animals in our books?"

Everyone nodded in agreement.

"I'll be back. I have to show you all the most adorable thing ever." I followed Troy out. Now I needed to remember to bring Murphy down when we came back.

We hurried up to Jerry's room, and Troy went in. I stood by the door for a few minutes, then he exited.

"It definitely looks the same as the money in the rain gutter."

"I'm going to try to get him to let me see his phone."

"Good idea."

"Let me grab Murphy." I grabbed him, and then we returned to the group.

"Oh my goodness!" Patty exclaimed. "He is sooo cute!" I handed him to her, and he licked her face. Patty was a dog fanatic, and she wasn't disgusted by anything they did. "Oh, baby, you are the sweetest thing!"

"That's Murphy," I said.

Patty held Murphy up so everyone could see him. "I hereby declare that Murphy is our mascot."

"Hear, hear!" Jim said, waving his cane in the air.

Patty cuddled him next to her face. "And he gets to sit with me today."

"What do we think about the book so far?" I asked. I'd already read all of it, but I had more self-control than Billie.

"I'm loving it," Lydia said. "I think I've almost figured out who the murderer is."

Billie rolled her eyes. "It's not very hard."

Jim glared. "Next time, read half of the book, and then we'll see if you really are as good at predicting the murderer as you think you are."

"Or you could tell us who killed Harrison," Roberta said, taking a sandwich.

The room went quiet for a moment.

Billie sniffed. "I probably could if someone told me all the information. Some people are a little tight-lipped." She glanced over at Troy, and he smiled. I wondered if she'd been trying to get information out of him.

"I bet Viola did it," Patty teased. "She's the maid here, right? Isn't it usually the maid?"

Viola put a hand to her forehead in dramatic style and tilted her head back. "Slander. And I'm not the maid.

That's so old-fashioned. I do housekeeping." She giggled. "And I only work here two nights a week for a couple of hours. That hardly qualifies as being the maid."

"Doesn't it freak you out, being around dead bodies?" Lydia asked.

Viola shrugged. "I only do quick run-throughs. Believe me, I'm in and out of the body storage room as fast as I possibly can."

"What about you?" Lydia asked me. "You live in a place full of bodies."

I shrugged. "I wouldn't say full of bodies. There's usually no more than two at a time."

"Still, isn't it scary?"

"I'm used to it."

"It never scares you?"

Troy grinned. "I remember when your grandpa would make you turn off the lights to the basement and you would almost have a panic attack."

I rolled my eyes. "That was ages ago, and I was a dramatic child."

Patty tilted her head. "You two knew each other as children?"

"Sure they did," Jim said. "Don't you remember when Neeley and her little friends were always running crazy around the town? They caused all sorts of trouble."

"Now that you mention it, I might. I didn't remember it was the sheriff."

Troy grabbed a sandwich. "I've reformed."

I gave Jim a playful glare. "Maybe the town should get a few things for kids to do." Jim was on the city council.

"Probably. We are talking about putting in a park."

"We have a park," Lydia said.

"I mean a park with a playground, not just grass."

"Are we ever going to talk about the book?" I asked. I didn't want anyone reminiscing about what delinquents we had been. I'd spent a lot of time trying to convince people I'd changed from my crazy teenage ways.

"Right, the book," Jessa said. "I can't wait to find out how it ends."

Chapter 14

"Uncle Jerry?" I went into the kitchen, where Jerry was eating a sandwich.

He glanced up but said nothing.

"My phone battery died. Can I use yours to call Grandpa?"

He sighed and pulled his phone from his pocket. He pushed in his password and handed it to me. "Make it fast."

"Thanks."

I stepped into the hallway and went to his texts. He had one labeled 'Harrison'. I opened it and my eyes scanned the message. I'd read this text before. Jerry was the person in Harrison's phone as 'the man'.

I put a hand to my forehead and closed my eyes. Not good.

I hurried and called my grandpa's number in case my uncle checked. He didn't answer, which made sense since he didn't have his phone. I returned the phone to my uncle.

"Did he answer?" he asked.

"No. They took his phone. I thought they would give it back, since no one thinks he's guilty anymore."

His brows met. "What do you mean? He looks completely guilty. I don't want to think of my dad as a murderer, but he was holding the gun."

I crossed my arms. "You think he's guilty?"

"Yep. Sorry, Neeley. I don't think he meant to do it, but he's getting older and not as good at thinking things through."

"Did you know Harrison?"

"A bit. I oversaw his work." He put down the sandwich as if my questions were inconveniencing him.

"Was he a good worker?"

He shrugged. "He was a slow digger, but I didn't have any complaints."

"You never saw him doing anything suspicious?"

"You're talking about the graves that were disturbed?"

I nodded.

"Nope. He must have been doing it at night if it was him."

"He must have had help." I couldn't think of a reason for Harrison to owe Jerry money, unless Jerry had been helping him. Jerry could have been hiding the stolen goods in the attic… It was the only thing that made sense. Except a woman had been up there.

"I think you're worrying too much," he said. "Leave it to the police."

"I know. I'm just ready for it all to be over. I'm going to talk to Grandpa. Do you want me to tell him anything?"

"Nope. I talked to him yesterday."

I nodded and collected Murphy from my room. I wasn't sure how he would do on a car ride, but I would give it a try. I knew Troy was in Crystal Rock doing some paperwork, and I wanted to tell him what I'd learned from Jerry's phone.

I opened the back door to the car and placed Murphy inside. He sniffed around while I made sure the little doggie booster seat I'd purchased online was secure. Murphy jumped up and sat inside the cozy box, and I made sure the tethers were all in place—and that he could still look out the window. I wondered if he'd done this before. He seemed to be a pro. Once I was sure he was secure, we drove toward Crystal Rock.

Every time I glanced in the mirror, Murphy was happily watching the scenery fly by. I'd believed he would hate the seat and refuse to cooperate, but he seemed to be a go-with-the-flow kind of dog.

At the police station, I made sure I was holding him, but the woman sitting behind the glass at the front desk gave me a glare. Her gray hair was pulled back into a no-non-sense ponytail, and she sucked in her already gaunt cheeks as she studied me.

"No dogs unless they are service dogs," she said. "No support animals."

"Sorry, I didn't know. I'm looking for Sheriff McGregor."

She looked me up and down. "I'm sure you are."

I raised my eyebrow. "Is he here? I have some information for him. I'd also like to speak with my grandpa. He's in the cell in the back."

"No dogs," she said again, her face letting me know she meant it. "Take him outside, and come back and tell me your problem, and I'll decide whether you need the sheriff."

"I can't leave him outside and I don't live in town."

"Not my problem."

"If I go out, will you tell the sheriff to come talk to me out there, please?"

Her eyes narrowed. "The sheriff is in charge. We don't tell him what to do."

I sighed. "He'll want to talk to me."

"Is it an emergency?"

"No, but—"

"Then get out. I'm tired of all the women coming in trying to get a glimpse of the sheriff. We don't have time for things like that."

I blinked. "That's not why—"

She stood. "I said out!"

I nodded and left the building. "She's fun," I said to Murphy. "Now what?" We went back to the car, and I put him inside, but left the door open. I pulled out my phone and called Troy. I probably should have done that before I came.

"Hello?"

"Hey, Sheriff. I'm outside your office. I have some information for you."

"Come inside."

"I have Murphy with me. I just got kicked out. I'm pretty sure the woman at the front desk hates me."

He laughed. "That's Martha. I guess you're the reason she's grumbling about women dropping by trying to seduce the sheriff."

"What? She's crazy."

"So that's not why you're here?" he teased.

"Not at all."

"Figures."

I rolled my eyes. "Are you coming out here or what?"

"Come back in."

"I can't leave Murphy."

"Bring him. I'll meet you."

I hung up and grabbed Murphy. It was good he was easygoing. We went back in, and Martha's eyes narrowed.

Troy came up from behind her. "It's okay, Martha." He opened a door to her side and motioned me to follow him.

"The dog's fine," Troy said. "He might be a witness."

I held in a smile when the woman glared at him. I followed Troy into his office and sat in a chair across from his desk.

"Sorry about that," I said. "I didn't think about what I would do with Murphy when I got here."

He sat on his chair. "It's fine. Martha is strict on rules. What's up?"

"I looked at Jerry's phone. He was the guy on Harrison's phone who was listed as 'the man.' I'm not actually surprised. That could mean he hid the stolen things in the attic, or told Harrison and Tori that they could do it, and showed them how to get up. I bet Harrison was going to pay him and that's what they were talking about."

Troy leaned back and nodded. "That makes sense."

"That makes me think Jerry didn't kill him. I was thinking about it on the way."

Troy tilted his head. "Why would you think that?"

"Because he had all that money under his mattress. I bet Harrison did pay him in the end."

"Or maybe, he killed Harrison, and took the money off him."

"But it was a woman who had his phone."

"Right... maybe they were working together."

"I'm not sure how much time they would have had to search the body. It sounds like Grandpa got in there pretty fast."

"Hmm. I'm going to have to think about it."

"Can I see my grandpa for a minute? I want to try to talk him into coming home."

He stood and came around his desk. "Sure. Let me go with you, I'll hold Murphy. No one will question me."

I handed him the pudgy pug, and he led me down the hall and to the cells. Grandpa was propped up on a big pile of pillows, watching a movie and eating popcorn.

"Why are you making him so comfortable?" I muttered.

Troy shrugged. "He's your grandpa. I don't want him to hate me more than he already does."

"Neeley!" Grandpa said, sitting up. "I thought you forgot about me."

"Nope. I think you should come home."

He glared at Troy. "Did you put her up to this? I'm staying here until I talk to my lawyer."

I sighed. "You don't need a lawyer. Come on. Think of all the business you're losing."

"Jerry can handle things."

"I haven't seen him do any work since you came here."

"He said he's been working nonstop."

"He lied."

"I'm sure you don't know what it takes to run a mortuary. He's probably doing things you don't understand."

Murphy barked.

"No dogs allowed," Grandpa said, glaring at Troy.

"He's mine," I said.

He ran a hand over his eyes. "Neeley, we can't have a dog."

"He's a good dog."

"That's what everyone says about their own dogs."

I rubbed Murphy's head. "But it's true. You'll love him."

"You can't keep a dog at the mortuary."

"Fine. I'll move."

His brows met in the middle. "Don't be like that. You don't have time for a dog. They need attention and more care than you can deal with."

"I'm not a kid, Grandpa. I can handle it."

"We'll talk about it later."

I leaned against the bars. "Are you coming home?"

"Not yet."

"Why? This doesn't make sense. If you want a vacation, go on vacation. This is just sad."

"I can get you a room at the hotel," Troy offered.

Grandpa grimaced. "I'm not staying at the hotel. Doesn't your buddy run the place?"

"Why does that matter?"

"Because I've been enjoying the last few years without the two of you around."

Troy smiled. "I tried."

I looked up at him. "Can you leave for a minute?"

"I'm not supposed to, but I guess it's okay since he shouldn't even be here." He stepped out the door and closed it.

Grandpa got up and walked over to me. "Just leave me for a few more days."

Serious conversations with my grandpa were never my thing, but I pressed my lips together and nodded. "Fine. But can I ask you something?"

He narrowed his eyes, wary. "What?"

"Could you be nice to Troy?"

He snorted. "Not after how upset he made you."

"It wasn't his fault," I said quietly. "Troy and Chase were the best friends I had back then. I was the one who pulled away."

Grandpa's expression softened. "You were a mess."

"Troy thought of me as a best friend. That's all. I was the one who wanted more. I made things messy."

Grandpa's eyes went wide. "Oh. And he rejected you? I knew he was a bum."

"No, he didn't. I didn't tell him. I don't want to talk about this, alright? He still doesn't know. Be nice to him, alright?"

There was a beat of silence. Grandpa studied me, his voice unusually gentle. "You still have feelings for him?"

I looked away. "It's been a long time."

"That's not a no."

"I don't want to talk about it," I muttered. "Just... please try to be civil. We're friends again, and I want to keep it that way."

"I'll try," he grumbled. "If it means that much to you."

"Thanks." I offered a small smile. "I hope you come home soon. I miss you."

"Yep."

I told myself that meant he missed me too. I couldn't believe I'd never told anyone about my feelings for Troy and I'd just told my grandpa. He wasn't someone I confided in.

Troy was in the hall talking to Murphy. He looked up when I came out. "Done?"

"Yes. Thanks."

"I'll walk you out."

We walked past Martha, and her nostrils flared.

When we got to my car, I took Murphy and put him in his seat. "I'm going to avoid this place. Martha does not like me."

He laughed. "Be glad you aren't McKenzie. Martha grabbed her by the arm once and physically escorted her from the building."

I grinned. "Let me guess. McKenzie came by hoping to seduce the sheriff?"

He smirked. "You know her. She used to show up weekly with lame excuses. I had to ban her from the building."

"I talked to her the other day. She told me she was dating someone. She always drove me crazy, but I feel a little bad for her."

"Why?"

"She was always after you and Chase. She didn't seem to like one of you over the other; she just hoped one of you would fall for her. It's a sad way to be." I couldn't imagine liking two guys at the same time. Especially two guys who couldn't stand me. "It had to all be based on looks. You guys were never nice to her."

Troy raised an eyebrow. "Are you saying I'm attractive?"

I punched him playfully on the arm. "Don't get a big head. You know McKenzie was completely superficial."

"I'm just glad she's finally moved on."

"What about Quincy? Is she still around?" Quincy had been as bad as McKenzie.

His jaw tightened. "You can Google her."

I blinked. "That bad?"

He nodded. "She's gone, though. I doubt she'll ever come back to Crystal Rock."

I glanced at Murphy. "I better go back to the flower shop. I've been neglecting it."

"I heard you have an online store now."

"Yeah. It's doing well. I could probably go all digital, but I like the shop."

Murphy barked. I figured that was my cue to go.

Chapter 15

"What do you think?" I asked Murphy. He stared at the gate I'd wrestled into place at the top of the stairs, then looked back at me. "Don't judge. It only took me an hour and three meltdowns."

Grandpa was going to freak when he saw the wall. I'd drilled two extra holes before getting it right. Maybe I'd have time to patch and paint later, but the whole thing had taken twice as long as planned.

"Now you can run all over this floor. You should be happy."

Murphy licked his nose and waddled off down the hall to my room. My next step would be a doggie door in my room. I gathered up my pink tools and put them in my toolbox, then went in my room and shoved them under the bed.

I hid them so Grandpa and my uncle didn't use them and gunk them up. I was picky about tools. Indoor ones stay pristine; outdoor ones are a disaster. Borrow the messy ones all you want, but touch my clean tools and I'd notice.

The doorbell rang, echoing around the large building. Grandpa put in a big doorbell system so it could be heard all over the place. I rushed down the stairs and opened the door. A delivery person stood there holding a bunch of balloons.

"Neeley Kelter?" he asked.

"That's me."

"Happy birthday," he said, handing me the balloons. It wasn't my birthday, but I figured the card attached to the balloons would clue me in to the real reason someone had sent them.

"Thank you." I took them and put them on the front desk. They had a small weighted circle attached to the bottom so they wouldn't fly away. I took off the envelope and pulled out a card. Inside was a gift card to a spa in the city and a note.

It read, *I figure you have enough flowers. I'm sorry for all your aches and pains. Thanks for all the help. Troy.*

Warmth spread through my chest. I wasn't a spa girl, but my back and shoulders were still sore from all the digging. I might actually use this. I'd never been to the spa, so I wasn't sure what to expect. Jessa would probably go with me if

I asked. Then I wouldn't be lost and possibly embarrass myself.

"Murphy?" I called as I went up the stairs. He ran over to the gate and barked. "Do you want to go to the shop?" He barked again, which I took to mean yes. I leaned over the fence and picked him up, and we made our way down the hill.

Jessa was inside the building, wiping down all the glass. With all the displays, we tended to need to do that a lot to get rid of fingerprints.

"I'm sorry," I said. "I didn't realize you came in today."

"That's alright," Jessa said. "I was talking to Ed."

"Um... that's nice."

Ed was Jessa's husband. He'd died years ago. She claimed he was always around talking to her. She used to talk about it more, but it had been a while.

She pointed at the counter. "There was a note on the door for you."

I pulled a note out of an envelope and read it out loud. "'Neeley, I need to talk to you. Meet me in the left tower. — Troy.'"

"Ooooh. A rendezvous in a tower. I like it."

"You know Troy and I aren't like that. Also, he didn't write this."

Her eyes went wide. "What do you mean?"

"I know his handwriting, and this isn't it. Not even close." Whoever had sent this hadn't even tried.

"Don't go," Jessa warned. "Call the sheriff."

I nodded and pulled out my phone and dialed him.

"Hi, Neeley."

"I just got a note from someone claiming to be you. It said to meet you in the left tower."

"Where are you?"

"The flower shop."

"Stay there. Don't go anywhere near the mortuary. I'll go."

"Don't go alone."

"I don't have anyone to spare right now. I'll be fine."

"Come get me first, I'll go with you."

"No, this is my job. Stay where you are, so I don't have to worry."

I sighed in frustration. "Are you in Crystal Rock?"

"No. I'm at the cemetery."

"Troy, do not go to the mortuary by yourself. Do you hear me?"

"Neeley, I have to. Someone is obviously setting something up."

"What if they want you to go? They didn't even try to use your handwriting. Maybe that was the point. To get me to call you so you'd walk into it."

"I'm trained. I have a gun."

"That doesn't mean you're invincible."

"Don't worry about me. Just stay put, I'll be over in a while."

"Troy!" I yelled as he hung up. "Troy! Dang it." I threw my phone onto the counter and turned to Jessa. "Watch Murphy."

Jessa shook her head. "I think you'd better listen to the sheriff."

"No, he's going to go walk into trouble."

"And you think it's better if you go too? He knows what he's doing."

"Troy is confident. Too confident. He's never had the sense to know he isn't invincible. I'm going." I hurried out the door before she could say anything and ran up the hill.

When I got to the mortuary and went into the lobby, I saw Troy standing by the stairs. He frowned at me. "I knew you would come."

I smiled. "I'll grab my bat."

"I want you to go back."

"And I want you to have backup."

"I can't."

"Then let's wait outside and see who comes out. They can't stay in here forever. While we're out there, you can call Chase. He can be your backup."

"Chase isn't trained for this."

"He can handle himself."

"So can I."

"Great. I'll handle it with you. If they said they are in the left tower, they are probably expecting someone to come in the right tower. If we climb up either one, someone could throw something down.”

“That’s what I’ve been thinking. I’ll go up first.”

“Or we could pull the fire alarm. That might get them out.”

Troy looked at the red handle on the wall; I could see the thoughts spinning in his head. “Let me call the fire department and tell them it’s only a drill.” He pulled out his phone and stepped away while he talked to someone.

There was more than one way out of the mortuary, but the front door was the most obvious. If the person knew the place well, they could go out the back door, but that would also require going past us in the lobby and down into the basement.

“Alright,” Troy said. “Do you want to pull it?”

I grinned and went over to the alarm. “You know I always have.”

He winked. “Do it.”

I pulled it and immediately covered my ears as a loud siren rang. Flashing lights spun and made me feel a little dizzy. Loud footsteps from the upper floor sounded, and Troy grabbed my arm and pulled me over to the corner behind a fake plant.

I watched through the leaves as Jerry tore down the steps, dressed all in black. He ran out the front door.

Troy looked at me and put a hand on my arm. “Are you going to be alright?”

"What do you mean?"

"It looks like it was Jerry."

"Maybe. He does live here. There might be someone else."

"Why would he be dressed like that?"

"Even if it was him, you know we've never been close."

He nodded, and we waited five more minutes before deciding no one else was in the house. Troy turned off the alarm, and we went outside.

Jerry was standing near a tree, looking at the side of the building. He didn't even see us come out.

"Jerry?" I called.

He jogged over. "The fire alarm went off, but I don't see any fire."

I spotted a gun in the back of his black jeans. I tried to motion with my head to alert Troy, but he narrowed his eyes in confusion.

I walked behind Jerry, grabbed the gun, and ran several paces off.

Jerry spun. "What are you doing?" He took a step toward me—until I raised the gun.

"What are you doing? You know I have a gun. I have a permit."

I glared. "Why did you leave me that note?"

Troy hurried to my side and took the gun from me. He pulled out his own gun, but didn't aim it.

"What note?" Jerry asked.

"The one telling me to go to the attic. Were you planning on shooting me, or did you think Troy would come?"

"I didn't leave you a note," he denied. "I wasn't going to shoot anyone."

"Why are you dressed like that? You never dress like that."

"Calm down," Troy muttered. "I've got this."

I shifted and waited. I didn't see what good doing things slowly would do.

"What's going on, Jerry?" Troy asked.

"Nothing. I don't know what you're talking about." He shifted from one foot to the other.

"Harrison wanted to dig up graves and find treasure," I said. "He needed somewhere to store things, and someone to turn a blind eye to what he was doing. He paid you to allow him to keep digging and store things in the attic."

Jerry swallowed hard and looked from side to side.

"Don't run," Troy said, raising his gun. "What were you planning to do today in the attic?"

"Nothing. None of this is true."

"You have the money Harrison paid you under your mattress," I said.

His eyes went wide. "What were you doing in my room? I didn't do anything wrong. Okay, I took some money... but that's not a crime, is it? I didn't kill anyone."

"Taking the money and allowing Harrison to continue was illegal," Troy said. He ran a hand over his head. "But it wasn't murder. What were you planning? You probably knew Neeley would recognize that note wasn't written by me, which means you wanted me to come."

"I wasn't going to do anything."

Troy pulled out his handcuffs and walked toward Jerry. I was ready to spring if I needed to.

Jerry sighed and held his hands up while Troy gave him his rights.

Troy's truck must've been at the cemetery, because he walked my uncle in that direction.

I followed after them, because I didn't trust Jerry, and I didn't want Troy to be alone with him.

"Who else was working with Harrison?" I asked.

"How should I know?" Jerry grumbled. "I wasn't in on everything he was doing. He probably wasn't stupid enough to tell people all of his plan."

"Did you ever meet his sister?"

"No."

"Are you sure?"

He glared over his shoulder. "I wasn't working with him. I only took money to look the other way."

"And let him stash his stuff in the attic."

"Why would I let him do that?"

I raised a brow. "Gee, Jerry. Maybe the cash under your mattress?"

"I don't know anything about that, or the murder."

"Sure you don't." I stretched out the word 'sure' with pure sarcasm.

"I'm not saying anything else without an attorney."

"Good idea," Troy said. "Now keep walking."

Chapter 16

Billie leaned her elbows on the counter in my flower shop. "I need a bright bouquet. Something eye-catching. And it has to last at least three days."

"What type?" I asked.

"I don't care. I just want it to be impressive. Nothing too green. I want it to catch people's eyes and make them ask about it."

"Are you having company?"

"Not that I've planned on, but you never know when someone might stop by. And I want a nice vase. A white one. You know the kind I'm thinking of? I don't want a clear glass one. That shows the water and isn't attractive."

"Got it," I said. "Want to wait, or come back for it?"

Murphy wandered lazily around the room, but Billie hadn't complained. Yet.

"I've got time. I'll wait."

Of course she would. I was skilled at making impressive bouquets, but it made me nervous when people stared at me while I did it, and Billie could watch something for a long time.

Troy hadn't called yet, and it had been three hours since he'd taken Jerry in. Jessa had already gone home, but I'd kept the shop open because Troy had asked me not to go to the mortuary without him. He wanted to check things and make sure it was safe.

Billie leaned forward. "I'm beginning to wonder if we should have a new place to meet for book club. A lot of dangerous stuff has been going down at your place."

"I'm hoping it will all be cleared up soon."

"Did we pick a book for tomorrow?"

I raised an eyebrow as I pulled out a white vase. "You mean you haven't already read it?"

"I've been busy."

"We're reading *A Witchy Mistake*, by Rhonda Hopkins."

"Oh right. It's the young adult series, correct?"

"Yes."

She smiled. "That means we get to dress up as witches. How fun. It's been a long time since I pulled out my witch hat. I better get my bouquet and hurry home to read. Sometimes a young adult book is just what I need."

I nodded and went over to my fresh flowers and looked them over. I had to admit, I liked a good YA book, and the chance to dress as a witch might be fun.

Once I was satisfied with the bouquet, I put it on the counter in front of Billie.

"I love the pinks," Billie said. "It's lovely. Do I get a discount?"

"Why would you?" I felt like we had this conversation at least once a month.

"Because it took you so long to make."

I gave her a look. I must've seemed annoyed, because she quickly pulled out her wallet and paid.

"See you tomorrow!" she said with a wave.

"Bye."

I went to the door and put the closed sign on it. Troy's truck drove up at the same time, so I hurried in, grabbed my things, and clipped Murphy's leash on his collar. We got out before Troy had exited the truck. He was still in the driver's seat, staring at his phone.

Now that we were friends again, I figured we could go back to how things used to be, so I got into the passenger's seat and put Murphy on my lap.

"How did it go?" I asked.

He sighed and put his phone down. "He admitted to a lot, but not the murder. Your grandpa wasn't happy to see him. I had to put a cell between them so they couldn't fight easily."

"Can't you force Grandpa to leave?"

"I normally would. If it were anyone else."

"You don't have to try to get on his good side by leaving him in jail."

Troy chuckled. "That was a strange sentence."

I smiled. "Well, Grandpa is a strange guy."

Murphy crawled off my lap and onto Troy's, then put his paws on the steering wheel.

"You don't have a license," Troy told him.

"He's so cute. He's getting a little smelly. How often do people give dogs baths? And do I do it, or pay someone else to do it?"

"I think every three to four weeks is normal. If you do it too often, they can get dry. You can do it yourself or pay someone. It's whatever you want."

"Did you bathe your own dogs?"

"Of course. You think my parents would spend money on a dog bath?"

I thought of his parents. There was no way. "I bet we don't have anyone around here who does it."

"Nope. The closest dog groomer is about an hour away. You should move to Crystal Rock. Then it would only be thirty minutes away."

"Do you have a dog?"

"No. Not since Sally died."

"She died?"

"Yeah. About ten years ago."

"I'm sorry."

"She was old. She had a good life." He shrugged. "It was rough on me, so I decided not to get another one."

"Do you still live with your parents?"

He rubbed Murphy's back. "No. They let me stay until I finished the academy, then I got an apartment near the police station."

"On the beach?"

"Almost. I can see the beach from my place, but it's down the road."

I tilted my head and looked at him. "I voted for you."

He gave me a half smile. "Did you now?"

"Yes. I'm sure that's why you were elected."

His smile grew. "Well, thanks. I appreciate it."

A car pulled up next to us, and I looked in the window. "It's Tori."

Troy unbuckled his seatbelt. "Oh, good. I thought she left town and I was going to have to put a warrant out for her." He moved Murphy off his lap and got out of the truck. I wanted to go as well, but I could occasionally stay out of things. I was hoping Troy would tell me what she said later.

She got out of the car and the two of them met and started talking. I didn't want to appear nosy, but I was definitely staring at them and wondering what they were saying.

She waved her hands around as she explained some-thing. Troy was nodding. Then Tori held her hand out, and Troy looked at it.

I really wished I could hear them. After a few minutes, she got back in her car and drove away.

Troy climbed back into the truck and shut the door.

"What was that all about?" I asked.

He huffed. "She wanted to tell me she helped Harrison dig up one grave. Tori said she thought it was legal because it was their ancestors' grave, and the stuff should belong to them. She said she only helped a little and left before he opened it, so she didn't even know what was inside. Harrison didn't pay her like he said he would, so she left town. He told her he would pay her later, and that's why she came back when she did."

"Do you think she was telling the truth?"

"I'm not sure. Her eye contact was atrocious. She also showed me her nasty fingernails to prove the one in the coffin wasn't hers."

"How would that prove it?"

"Because her real nail was still attached. But I'm not to-tally convinced. The fake one was small, jagged, and weird. Do you know what it looks like when fake nails come off?"

"No. I don't have the patience for something like fake nails. I have things to do and I don't need long nails getting in the way."

"I still kinda think she's guilty. It's hard to say. I wish the people would get back to me with the results of the fingernail. They seem to be taking their time."

"Have you gotten a warrant for the phone yet?"

"No. I'm hoping that will happen today."

"I should have looked at it more thoroughly. Did you read the book for book club tomorrow?"

"No. Now that no one in there is a suspect, I don't have time for it."

I tried to hide my disappointment. "But you would get to dress up like a witch."

He smiled. "How fun. If I get time, I'll come by. But I'm not dressing like a witch."

"Patty's making scones and honey butter."

"Ooh. I'll try harder to swing by. Will there be hot chocolate?"

"Of course."

Troy could drink hot chocolate in any temperature. He said some foods just needed to be eaten with it. I hadn't planned on having it, but if it brought him here, I'd stock up.

Pathetic. I'd walked right back into the same situation. Best friends with the guy I love. It was fine. I'd realized over the last fifteen years that it was better to be with Troy and not have him love me than to be without him.

"What are you thinking?" he asked. "You got serious."

I smiled. "Nothing important."

"Are you dressing like a witch?"

"Of course."

"Will Jim?"

I laughed. "I doubt it. He only dresses up occasionally. Patty, Lydia, and Viola are the only ones who dress up every time, but more and more people are starting to. It makes it fun."

"I won't have time to read the book."

"That's alright."

Murphy had fallen asleep by my feet, and he snored loudly. "I better take Murphy home. Is it okay to go back?"

"Yes. I ran over and looked through the attic and all around."

"Do you think Jerry was planning on shooting one of us?"

"I'm not sure, and since he isn't talking, we might never know."

"I'm not sure what he would accomplish. Killing one of us would make him look guilty of Harrison's murder as well."

"I feel like it will all come together soon," he said. "I keep thinking I'm almost there, then something else happens."

When I got home, I carried a sleeping Murphy up to his bed and gently put him down. Then I looked around my room and sighed. I'd been perfectly content living in the mortuary until the last few weeks. Now I was beginning to feel like it was too gloomy and too big.

If more people lived here, it might be better. Everyone was in jail or gone. I prided myself on not needing people, but I suddenly felt needy. What I felt needy for, I wasn't exactly sure.

Murphy rolled over and fell onto the floor. "You are not the most graceful dog."

He stood up and wandered lazily over to me.

"Do you want to go for a walk? You've been sitting a lot."

I wanted to go down to the cemetery and see if everything had been put back to normal. It had been days since I'd seen it.

Murphy and I entered the cemetery, and I was surprised to see the crime tape gone. There was still rope blocking off the graves that needed to be reburied, but the police had cleaned everything else up, and there was no one here. Everything valuable must've been gone.

Murphy pulled me toward a tree and then sat on the grass. I sank down next to him and leaned on the trunk. "It's going to be dark soon," I told him. "I might not freak out about dead bodies, but I do not like to be in the cemetery at night if I don't have to be."

Murphy rolled over and scratched his back on the grass. He didn't look in a hurry to get anywhere. It was fine. We could stay for a while longer.

A figure in a dark blue hoodie slipped into the cemetery, and I froze. People visited graves. That wasn't odd. It was odd to wear a big hoodie with the hood up when it was nice out though. He hadn't turned in my direction, so I crawled around to the other side of the tree, and Murphy followed me. We'd be safe if he didn't bark.

I peeked around the tree and watched the man go under the rope barrier and stand in front of one of the graves. When he turned to the side, I took a breath. It was Mitchel. What would he be doing out here? He had to know that anything valuable was gone at this point.

He didn't look into the graves, he just looked at the tombstones. He took out his phone and took a picture.

"Let's go," I whispered to Murphy, gripping his leash tightly as we crept away. I couldn't think of why Mitchel would take pictures of the graves, but I doubted anything he was doing was innocent. The rope was obviously up to keep people out.

I couldn't sleep that night, because I was wondering what he'd been doing. It baffled me trying to think of crimes that would involve taking a picture. I should have stayed longer to see if he did anything else. I'd texted Troy and let him know, and he couldn't think of what he might've been doing either.

It was good I wasn't normally involved in things like this. I wondered how Troy ever slept.

Chapter 17

I cringed as I stared into my full-length mirror. I wasn't sure I could go down to book club looking like this. I'd overdone the makeup, and the dress? Oh, the dress. It was perfect. I looked great clear from the tip of my pointed witch hat to my black high heels.

"This is pathetic, Murph. I look like I'm trying to catch a man."

I was pretty sure the look on Murphy's face was his way of saying, 'Well, aren't you?'

"No, I'm not," I said, not convincing anyone. "I just want to dress up for book club. Did I drive over two hours this morning to find the perfect witch costume? Yes, I did. But I did it for me. If Troy notices, that's not my fault." If he even came.

Murphy tilted his head and sneezed.

I covered my face with both hands. "Yes, I know, I'm pathetic."

I wasn't usually the person to choose a costume like this. I usually chose the dress that swept across the floor and swished when I walked, but this one came to my knees. I'd pulled on tights to hide the massive bruise on my leg. The dress was perfectly decent, but a lot more alluring and clingier than my usual style.

"It's time," I muttered. "No time to change. Come on, Murphy. I think people are expecting you."

We went to the book club room, and I tried to act natural as I entered. Jim, Patty, Jessa, and Roberta were already there. Jim was the only one who hadn't dressed up.

"Wow!" Jessa said. "That's some costume."

I pushed my hair over my shoulder dramatically. "Why thank you." My long dark hair worked better as witch hair than flapper hair.

Roberta adjusted her purple and black dress. "I need to get a new costume. I've had this one for at least a decade."

Jessa nodded. "I'm telling you, girl. I will take you and help you get a perfect new wardrobe. Witch outfit included."

"I know. I should take you up on it. I just find shopping so boring."

"Check out my tights," Jessa said, showing me her webbed tights. "Perfect, right?"

"I think so."

Lydia came in, wearing both a long black witch dress and hat.

Patty was making sure her scones were neat on the table.

"Oh! I need to get the hot chocolate," I said. "I'll be back." I hurried to the kitchen, grabbed the milk and chocolate powder, and took them back to the room. I had set the hot chocolate maker up earlier.

I poured in the milk and measured out chocolate, then pushed the button. It made the hot chocolate scalding, but something about making it in there made it taste better. It was probably all in my head.

"Hello, my dears!" Viola said, drifting into the room. Her witch dress had lights underneath it. No one could ever outdo Viola and her costumes. Her short hair was flipped out with the tips touching her lacy witch hat. She straightened her long black gloves and sat down.

"Who are we waiting on?" I asked.

"Billie," Jim said. "Geneva couldn't come today."

"Pity," Jessa said, "she loves when we read paranormal mysteries."

"I'm here!" Billie said, hurrying in. She was wearing a pink dress and a golden high crown. "I'm the witch from *The Wizard of Oz*. Can you tell?"

"Nice," I said. She sat down and Patty passed around small plates.

"What did we think of the first half of *A Witchy Mistake*?" Jim asked. "I'll tell you what I thought. I love the grandma. Who's with me?"

"Oh, me!" Jessa said. "I love an old lady who wants to hex everyone."

"You know I'm all about romance, and I sense some coming in future books," Roberta said. "I'm team Jackson. She mentioned a few attractive boys in the first half, but he has my vote."

"Since it's a young adult book, you might be disappointed," Viola told her.

"I don't need anything spicy. I like a cute, cozy romance. I actually prefer it."

Billie straightened her crown. "What about Nate? I like a man with some muscle."

Jim snorted, and we all laughed.

"How many books are out?" Roberta asked. "I'm going to finish the series after I read this one."

I shrugged. "There were a few, plus some on pre-order, if I remember right."

"I wish I liked reading on my phone. It would make getting books so much faster."

"Can we go back to the grandma?" Jim asked. "All books need a character like her. A little sassy, maybe a little crazy, but not too prevalent."

"I think an important part of the story is about Charley not having magic in a magic family," Patty said. "I mean, can you imagine how ripped off you would feel if you were the only one who couldn't do magic? She takes it better than I would."

Roberta nodded. "That would be my luck."

I stood and went to check the hot chocolate maker. "The hot chocolate is ready. Be careful though. It's super hot."

"Yes, you are," Troy said from the doorway.

I wanted to smile, but I rolled my eyes. "Come join us, Sheriff."

He entered and sat down. "I didn't read the book."

"That's alright," Patty said. "You can read it today or tomorrow and be ready next time. It's a quick, fun read." She handed him a plate and a small bowl of honey butter.

I grabbed a Styrofoam cup, filled it, then put it in front of him. I realized how that might look, so I got some for everyone else in the group.

"Patty, that is the best scone I've ever tasted," Troy said. He took another bite.

She beamed. "I should be good after all the years of cooking I've done." Patty and Lydia started talking about baking.

We never stayed on the subject long. We always slipped into talking and then someone had to get us back to order.

I sat next to Troy, and he leaned close to me. "The fingernail isn't Tori's," he whispered.

My brow furrowed. "How is that possible?"

He shrugged. "It didn't match anything in the database."

"That blows all my theories. We need to look at the phone again."

"I think that will get approved anytime." He grinned. "You know you look bewitching in that costume?"

"Ha ha. Eat your scone."

"Yes, ma'am." He took a big bite.

"Gross. I got honey on my glove," Viola said, pulling off the long glove.

My heart began pounding as I looked at her mocha mousse fingernails.

"Do you see that?" I whispered.

Troy wiped his mouth. "What?"

Viola wadded up the glove and put it in her purse. Tori said it was one of the most common colors of the year, and Viola's fingernails looked perfect. If I could just get her to take off the other glove...

"You should take off the other glove," I said. "You don't want to make the other one sticky."

Viola smiled. "I love my gloves, but you're right." She pulled the other one off and I glanced at her hand. No broken nails.

"What is it?" Troy whispered.

"Nothing."

"Oh, I didn't tell you! I brought your grandpa home. He's taking a shower."

"Thank goodness. I appreciate it." I exhaled. At least the house would feel less lonely.

"So back to the grandma," Jim said. "Best character."

"You already said that," Billie added. "I think Jim has a character crush."

"I do not. That's ridiculous."

"We're halfway through the book," Billie said. "Who thinks Charley's cousin is guilty?"

"I'm not sure," Lydia said. "She was definitely not being nice at the beginning."

Jessa nodded. "Yeah, but for good reason. She was being bullied. Why would she be nice to a school bully? I would have loved to have magic back when I had bullies, and I thought it was hilarious the way she dealt with it."

"It's not going to be the cousin," Jim said. "If it was, there wouldn't be a mystery."

"I like how the family is close," Roberta said. "They all believe the cousin is innocent because they have family loyalty. She looks guilty, but they know she wouldn't do it, even though she has a slight temper."

"Do you think Charley will ever get powers?" Viola asked. "I hope she does."

"She's dressed like a witch on the cover, so maybe?" Troy said.

I tilted my head. "You said you didn't read it yet."

He grinned. "No, but I bought the book. I saw the cover. Sorry, just trying to participate."

"I like the pace," Viola said. "We should read more young adult books."

Jessa held her book in the air. "I agree. Do you think Jackson will find out Charley's family are witches?"

"I hope so," I said. "But not until they fall in love."

"*If* they fall in love," Patty corrected me.

"Fine, *if*. It's like on *Sabrina the Teenage Witch*. Didn't everyone always want Harvey to find out Sabrina was a witch?"

"He did like a million times," Roberta said. "He just got his memory erased."

I nodded. "And it drove me crazy. If I were a witch, I would want my boyfriend to know."

Jessa laughed. "Your boyfriend?"

A smile tugged at my lips. "Okay, so there are a lot of unbelievable things going on in my statement."

"I'd say Neeley is more likely to be a witch than have a boyfriend," Roberta teased.

I laughed. "True."

"Why are you so anti-dating?" Viola asked.

"I've got reasons."

"Let's hear them." Troy said, giving me a half smile.

"This is not the time."

"When will it be the time?"

"Probably never." I stared at Viola for a moment. I knew I was probably being ridiculous, but I moved across the room and bumped her purse onto the floor. "Oops. Sorry."

Her eyes narrowed quickly, then she smiled. "No problem." She leaned over to pick it up and I spotted the bruise on her neck. I looked closer at her nails.

My breath caught. The nail. The bruise. The gloves. Everything clicked into place. "Viola killed Harrison," I said.

The room went quiet, then Patty laughed. "Didn't we joke about that last time?"

I moved over near Troy. "Yes, but this time it's not a joke."

"I don't even know him," Viola said. "Why would I kill him?"

"You did know him. You dated him." I had absolutely no evidence of that, but I was guessing she was 'hottie' in his phone.

She smiled and shook her head. "That's a really weird thing for you to think."

"The evening Harrison was shot, you were here. You said you went to the bathroom, but my grandpa was in the bathroom, and he didn't see anyone. You were also wearing gloves, like usual, so your prints wouldn't have been on the gun."

"I work here. I know where all the bathrooms are, so I went to one that wasn't occupied."

"There is only one bathroom easily accessible when you're on this floor."

"Why would I leave book club to go to the bathroom, go into Walt's office, and shoot someone? I wouldn't have known there was a gun in there, or a person."

"What happened to your neck?" I asked.

"I don't know what you mean."

"You have a big bruise on your neck. Someone attacked me in the attic. I threw a rock and hit them in the neck."

She touched her neck. "Why would I be in your attic? That doesn't make sense."

"Every time someone trespassed, there was no sign of any forced entry. Most of the times the front door was unlocked, but a few times, it wasn't. You have keys to everything here."

I glanced at Troy. He nodded for me to go on.

"Then there was a fake fingernail in a coffin. You were helping Harrison dig up graves."

"I would never do that, and none of my nails are broken."

"On your right hand, one of the nails is newer than the others. All the rest are beginning to grow out, but not that one."

Viola looked around and smiled at everyone. "I think someone added something to Neeley's hot chocolate."

Everyone just stared.

She twisted her hands around each other. "Come on, you guys. You know it wasn't me."

"It won't be hard to determine some of it," Troy said. "The fingernail we found had blood on it. That makes it easy to identify."

Viola grabbed her hat and tossed it on the table. "Okay, fine, look." She sighed. "I might have helped Harrison dig up a few graves. All that stuff should have been his, anyway. It belonged to his family. When I pulled on the lid, my hand slipped and it ripped off my nail. That doesn't make me a murderer."

"What about attacking me in the attic?" I asked.

She sat and silently glared at me.

"How did she know about the attic?" Troy asked. "You didn't even know all the ways to get up."

"She cleans the rooms. She must have discovered it when she was cleaning, although I believe you were told to ignore the closets."

Viola stood and grabbed her purse. "Everything you're saying is a guess. You can't prove anything but that I helped with the grave."

"Let me see your phone."

"No."

"You threatened Harrison in a text. I saw it. You also stole Harrison's phone, because you dropped it when you were attacking me in the attic."

"I was only trying to find something of mine up there. You scared me!"

"You can't sneak into a place to find something. That's illegal."

She pointed at her neck. "Look what you did to me! I could sue you."

"Do you want to see the bruise on my shin from where you hit me with a baseball bat? It's much more impressive."

"What were you trying to find?" Troy asked.

"Just something I lost."

"Probably that piece of jewelry we found," I told him. "The one with the missing stones."

He nodded.

"It was mine. Not something stolen."

"And it was in my attic because...?"

"Who cares? I did some stuff. Lock me up, fine, but not for murder."

"You made me think my grandpa was losing his mind because you were sneaking around. Were you stealing things as well?"

"No. I was just helping Harrison. I knew no one went into the attic, so I figured he could hide stuff up there and it wouldn't hurt anything."

"How long did you date him?" Troy asked.

She scowled. "We weren't exactly dating. Not officially."

"But you were willing to dig up graves with him?"

"He made me believe I mattered. That we were partners. Then he ghosted me like I was nothing."

"And you killed him?" Jim asked.

"No, I told you, I didn't kill him." Viola threw her arms up in frustration.

"You left the room at the time he was killed. With everything else you said, I think you're guilty."

She pointed at him. "No one asked your opinion, Jim."

"But this is what we talk about in book club," Patty said, "and you sure seem guilty."

"Nothing I did was that bad."

"It's a federal offense to dig up a grave," Troy said. "You could go to jail for a long time, just for that. And then there is breaking and entering, and attacking someone."

"I'm leaving. This is ridiculous," she said. She turned and rushed out of the room.

Troy stood, leaped onto the table, and then to the floor, and ran after her.

I hurried around the table and scurried into the hallway just in time to see Troy grab her around the waist and pull her to a stop.

"Let go!" she said, beating on his arm with her fists.

He grabbed her hands and pulled them around behind her. He grabbed his handcuffs from the back of his belt and cuffed her using one hand. I was impressed.

"Nice job, Sheriff!" Jessa called from down the hall.

"I am going to sue everyone!" Viola yelled.

"You can talk to your lawyer about that," Troy said, unconcerned.

"There is absolutely nothing pointing to me killing him."

"You had Harrison's phone," I said.

"You don't know that."

"I'm sure it has your prints," Troy said.

"It was self-defense," she said as Troy led her down the hall.

"Oh?"

She was red in the face, and her pupils had blown. The small chase must've had her adrenaline pumping as everything slipped out in a panic. "I saw Harrison and followed him into Walt's office. He threatened me, so I grabbed the gun to defend myself. He came at me, I shot at him. I had to."

"Did he have a weapon?" I asked.

"I don't know."

"You could have yelled for help. There were a lot of people here," I added.

"Harrison had done a lot of illegal things. No judge was going to side with him," Troy pointed out.

I glared at her. "I bet you were just mad he hadn't paid you."

"Even if I was, isn't that still his crime? He owed me money, and he didn't pay."

Troy led her to the stairs. "Telling a judge you killed someone because they didn't pay you for helping them commit a crime isn't going to help your case."

"I never said I killed him. I'm only saying no one would blame me if I did."

"You missed the spot where you were supposed to stop talking and demand a lawyer," Jim said. "And you did say you killed him. You must be getting forgetful."

I led everyone back to the room, and we all sat quietly at the table for a moment.

"Well, that was the most excitement our group has ever seen," Jessa said.

Patty nodded. "Yes, but if anyone was going to turn out to be a killer, my money would have been on Viola. Remember that time when she jumped on Pearl Jorgensen's back and pulled her hair because Pearl won the silent auction at the town picnic?"

Jim chuckled. "And people say small towns are boring."

Roberta grinned at me. "Too bad we didn't video that. It would have gone viral, the way the sheriff jumped over the table, and you went running after in your witch costume."

I nodded. It had probably looked crazy. I sank into my chair, heart still racing. Solving the mystery didn't make the world right again, but it was a start.

Chapter 18

"This is a lot to take in," Grandpa said.

I shifted on the couch and patted his hand. "I'm sorry about Jerry."

He shrugged. "It's not that surprising. You should have seen that boy in high school. He was trouble. I know he's skimmed some money from me over the years, but I always looked the other way. I guess I should be glad he's not the murderer."

"There are other things we need to talk about. Your retirement, for one."

"I can't retire. Now things will be even crazier without Jerry here."

Murphy jumped up with his front paws on my leg, so I picked him up. "You've been working your entire life. You have plenty of money saved. It's time to at least slow down. You need to hire more people."

"It's a family business."

"Yes, well, we can't handle it alone. I'm not taking on Jerry's old jobs. I have too much with the flower shop."

"I suppose I could hire more people. It might be hard to find anyone though. This isn't a bustling town."

"Well try. I also think we should do a remodel on a lot of the rooms here."

"Why? What's wrong with the way it is?"

I looked around our dark living room and frowned. All the furniture was dark brown. The curtains were brown, the walls were gray. The floor had dark gray tile. Grandpa didn't care about matching, and he liked dark colors.

"It's dreary, I'm getting tired of looking at the dark colors all the time."

"Your room is brighter."

"Yes, but the rest of the place is horrid. People shouldn't have to come here and feel like they walked into a haunted house. They're already depressed enough if they have to be here. I'm going to make some huge flower arrangements to go on the front desk. That will help."

"I hate having flowers in the mortuary. The smell gives me a headache."

"People expect flowers. I'll use fake flowers. You should go to the city and look at other mortuaries. They are welcoming. You only do well because you have no competition."

"Fine. Do what you want," he grumbled.

I smiled. "I will."

"If you sold the flower shop, we wouldn't have to hire anyone else."

"Not going to happen."

"Trusting people who aren't family can bite you. We only have a handful of employees, and one of them turned out to be a graverobber, and one a murderer."

I tilted my head. "Yes, but your own son was involved in it all."

"I suppose."

"What if we ask Jessa to be the receptionist? It would be nice to have someone sitting at the desk when people come in. They can also keep an eye on things. I know she needs more hours, and I can't give them to her at the shop. She could be at the shop in the morning and here in the afternoon. You trust Jessa."

"I guess it wouldn't hurt to ask. And what about that dog?"

I looked down at Murphy. "What about him?"

"You're going to let him run all over the place?"

"Only upstairs. That's why I put the gate up."

Murphy climbed off me and over to Grandpa. I held my breath. Grandpa had never been an animal person. He put one paw on his leg, and Grandpa sighed and ran his hand over Murphy's back.

"I'll tolerate him."

I smiled. That might be the best I'd get. "Great. I'm meeting Troy for lunch. I'll see you soon."

"Is it a date?"

"Not at all. He has some things he wants to tell me about the case."

"I'll watch the dog."

"His name is Murphy."

"Fine. *Murphy* and I are going to watch TV."

"Great." I hoped Grandpa would bond with Murphy. It would be good for him.

By the time I got to the diner, Troy was already there, and he was sitting with Mitchel Nance. They were both staring at a laptop.

I sat across from them. "Hello," I said, dropping my purse next to me. "What's going on?"

Mitchel smiled and turned the laptop to face me. "You opened my eyes to family history."

I raised my brow. "Oh, yeah?"

"When you brought up my ancestors and then the sheriff showed me the way I was related to the Brightmans, I got excited and started studying my family tree. There are so many online resources, I've learned a ton."

"That sounds fun."

"Yeah, I found out that not only was I related to rich people like the Brightmans, I also had ancestors who came over on the Mayflower with almost no money at all. I even found a site someone had scanned my fourth great-grand-father's journals onto."

I rested my chin on my hand. "Interesting. Is that why you were taking pictures of the Brightman graves?"

"Yeah. Sorry I went in there, Sheriff. I scanned the pictures and put them on some of the sites so other people I'm related to can find them. I'm thinking of starting a website dedicated to the Brightman family. I've connected to a bunch of people all over the country who are third and fourth cousins."

"That's really neat. What's going to happen to all the jewels from the graves?" I asked. I couldn't believe the change in Mitchel. I didn't realize he could get excited.

Troy cleared his throat. "We're not going to rebury it. It's too much of a temptation for robbers and doesn't serve a purpose. Once they're released as evidence, it'll be split between all the direct living relatives. They can keep it or donate it."

I nodded.

Mitchel looked at his hands. "I'm sorry about all the trouble my siblings caused. I feel bad about the way Harrison ended, but he's always been headed for some kind of terrible end. I guess Tori will go to jail for all the stuff she did."

Troy nodded. "Probably. Graverobbing is a serious crime, and she helped trash Neeley's store."

I frowned. I hadn't heard that Tori had been involved in that.

"Yeah, well, I'm going to move back to San Diego," Mitchel said. "I'm not cut out for small-town life." He stood and shook my hand, then Troy's. "You have my number if you need anything." He grabbed his laptop and left.

"That was the most pleasant I've seen him," I said.

Troy leaned back. "Yeah, he's pretty excited about all that family stuff. Maybe because the family he knows is dysfunctional."

"What did you mean by Tori and my shop?"

"When Tori was being questioned, she said that wrecking the shop was Viola's idea. I guess the two of them were friends through Harrison, and Viola thought it would take eyes off the morgue. The two of them did it together."

"Unbelievable," I muttered. "Anything else?"

"The jeweled hair clip you found in the attic was something Harrison gave Viola. It was in her hair when she went to book club, it fell out when she killed Harrison. She grabbed it and didn't notice that two of the gems had fallen out. She put it in her pocket and lost it again when she was in the attic."

"She should reconsider where she puts things. She lost the clip and the phone. Has she confessed?"

"Yes. I convinced her it would go easier on her, and I told her about the gems from the clip that were found at the murder scene."

My eyes narrowed. "You found them? Why didn't I know?"

He grinned. "You don't work for me."

"I thought you'd told me everything."

"Not everything."

"Was the hair clip from a grave?" I asked.

"No, and it was a cheap piece of garbage. That's why it fell apart so easily. Viola was steaming mad when she found out it was fake. I guess she started dating Harrison a few months ago. He didn't want anyone to know, so they kept it secret."

"Why would you date someone who didn't want anyone to know? That is such a red flag."

"Seriously," he agreed and continued, "he got her to help him, then she got angry when he didn't pay her. She saw him go into Walt's office. He'd been avoiding her, so she went in to confront him. I'm not sure exactly what happened, but he made her mad and she grabbed the gun. Keep this all quiet for now. It will all come out soon enough."

"Okay."

"We also found a bunch of stuff that Viola had stolen from the mortuary while she was working there."

"I feel bad that I told Grandpa he was imagining things." I slumped in my chair.

"We all thought he was. I'll make sure he gets everything back. It looks like she was stealing before she even met Harrison."

"I've convinced Grandpa to hire more people. I'm hoping I can get him to hire enough people that he can be the boss and not actually do anything."

"Walt has always been a hard worker."

"He is."

"Is he going to let you keep Murphy?"

"Yes. I keep wondering if I should move. At thirty-five, I shouldn't have to ask my grandpa if I can have a dog."

"Where would you go?"

"I'm not sure. I probably won't move. Grandpa needs me. I might have to tell him he has to let me have more say in some things."

"You've never let him boss you around."

"No, but I've respected things like the no pet rule. He needs me, so he needs to let me have things I need."

"We found Tennison's body."

My eyes went wide. "Where?"

"Viola's trunk."

"But why?"

"There was a ton of jewelry on the body. My guess is they were running out of time, so they grabbed it and hid it so they could deal with it later."

"If Viola had all that jewelry, why be mad at Harrison for not paying her? It had to be worth a lot."

"From what I understand, she was too unsettled to touch the skeleton. She was mad that Harrison put it in her trunk."

"She helped steal it, but was too scared to get the loot? Unbelievable."

The waiter came over and took our orders. I never even looked at the menu. It was small and I had it memorized. I ordered grilled cheese and fries, and Troy ordered fried chicken.

"One good thing came from this mess," he said.

"Murphy?"

He winked. "Okay, two things. I'm glad we're friends again."

I smiled and tilted my head. "Me too. Thanks for forgiving me and my fifteen-year, uncalled-for grudge."

Troy shrugged. "I understand where you were coming from. I'm just sorry I didn't hunt you down and force you to listen to me."

"I did my best to not listen. Chase even tried a few times, and I wouldn't listen to him."

"We all make mistakes."

"Do you think Chase will forgive me?"

"One hundred percent."

"Do you still spend a lot of time together?"

"Yeah, but it's not like we used to. He's married now, and we're both busy. I eat dinner with him and his wife most nights."

"Third wheel, huh?" I teased.

He took a sip of water. "It's not that bad. There's another person who eats there."

I tried not to look uneasy. Did he have a girlfriend? We hadn't talked about that. "Who is it?"

"An old security guard."

"I see. That's not pathetic or anything. I thought you were going to say you had a girlfriend."

He smiled. "I'll have you know I have plenty of women who want to date me. I'm just too busy."

"Hmm."

"You don't believe me?"

"If you wanted to date, you could. You have time to eat at Chase's every night, so you could date during that time."

"That's what Chase says, but I have to eat. I don't hang around for a long time after. Besides, it's been a while since I've met anyone I wanted to date."

I nodded and unwrapped my straw. "Well, I hope you can find time to hang out every now and then."

"I'm sure I can." He sounded almost gentle. "What about Chase?"

I stuck the straw in my water. "Can I wait to talk to him for a while? I know I need to apologize, but I want to wait until I think about it."

"That's fine. Whenever you're ready. Maybe we can all go up to the attic and finish that board game we started fifteen years ago."

I laughed. "How will we know whose piece is whose?"

"Easy. You were always red, I was green, and Chase was blue."

"I guess we were predictable. You're always welcome at book club as well."

"I might be able to swing some of those. They're late enough in the evening I could probably drop by once or twice a month."

The waiter brought our food, and I hoped I wasn't smiling like an idiot. I had a feeling my life was taking a turn for the better, and I couldn't wait to see what bloomed next.

Watch for Murder Among the Moonflowers to continue Neeley's journey!

Also By Kristy Dixon

<u>Cozy Mystery</u>
Murder With a Side of Bacon
Murder With a Hint of Cinnamon
Murder With a Fudge Brownie to Go
Murder With a Splash of Vanilla
Murder With a Drizzle of Syrup
Murder With a Slice of Pie
Murder With a Swirl of Blueberry
Murder With a Bite of Biscotti
Murder With a Sip of Eggnog
Suite Lies and Alibis

Not So Suite Caroline
A Suite Case of Murder
Peril Among the Pansies
Murder Among the Moonflowers

<u>Young Adult</u>
The Silver Eclipse (3 books)
The Amethyst Crown
More Than Once Upon a Time
Trapped In Once Upon a Time
The Beginning of Once Upon a Time
Riviand Lost (5 books)

<u>Coming Soon!</u>
Lies Among the Lilies
Marrying My Prickly Boss

About the Author

Kristy Dixon started writing stories at age seven and never stopped. These days, she writes cozy mysteries full of quirky characters, small-town charm, and the occasional dead body. She also writes YA novels when the teens in her head get too loud to ignore. Kristy lives with her husband, kids, one spoiled cat, and a flock of chickens who think they run the place. When she's not writing or wrangling her crew, she's likely playing board games, plotting murders (fictional, of course), or dreaming about cookies.

www.ingramcontent.com/pod-product-compliance
Lightning Source LLC
Chambersburg PA
CBHW031528310726
48971CB00008B/2392